PANCHATANTRA
51 SHORT STORIES WITH MORAL (ILLUSTRATED)

BY PANDIT VISHNU SHARMAN

ILLUSTRATED & EDITED BY PRAFUL B, MAHARSHI G FROM VYANST

Panchatantra – 51 short stories with Moral (Illustrated)
By Pandit Vishnu Sharman
Illustrated by Praful B, Maharshi G from Vyanst
Copyright © 2013 Vyanst

TABLE OF CONTENTS

CHAPTER 1

PANCHATANTRA

Once upon a time, King Amarasakti ruled the city of Mahilaropyam in the south of India. He had three witless sons who became a matter of endless worry for him. Realizing that his sons had no interest in learning, the king summoned his ministers and said: "You know I am not happy with my sons. A son who is stupid will bring dishonor to his father. "

How can I make them fit to be my successors? I turn to you for advice.

One of the ministers suggested the name of Vishnu Sharman, a great scholar enjoying the respect of hundreds of his disciples.

"He is the most competent person to tutor your children. Entrust them to his care and very soon you will see the change."

The king summoned Vishnu Sharman and pleaded with him "Oh, venerable scholar, please train my sons into great scholars and I will make you the lord of hundred villages."

Vishnu Sharman said "Oh, king, listen to my pledge. Hundred villages do not tempt me to vend learning. Count six months from today. If I do not make your children great scholars, you can ask me to change my name."

The king immediately called his sons and handed them to the care of the learned man. Sharman took them to his monastery where he started teaching them the five strategies (Panchatantra). Keeping his word, he finished the task the king entrusted him in six months. Since then, Panchatantra has become popular all over the world as a guide to solving problems of life.

Pancha means five and tantra means systems or strategies.

The five strategies are
First Strategy: The Gaining of Friends
Second Strategy: Discord among Friends
Third Strategy: Of Crows and Owls
Fourth Strategy: Loss of Gains
Fifth Strategy: Imprudence

CHAPTER 2

THE FOUR FRIENDS AND THE HUNTER

Long, long ago, there lived three friends in a jungle. They were a deer, a crow and a mouse. They used to share their meals together. One day, a turtle came to them and said, "I also want to join your company and become your friend. I'm all alone."

"You're most welcome," said the crow. "But what about your personal safety. There are many hunters around. They visit this jungle regularly. Suppose, a hunter comes, how will you save yourself?"

"That is the reason why I want to join your group," said the turtle

No sooner had they talked about it than a hunter appeared on the scene. Seeing the hunter, the deer darted away. The crow flew in the sky and the mouse ran into a hole. The turtle tried to crawl away fast, but he was caught by the hunter. The hunter tied him up in the net. He was sad to lose the deer. But he thought, it was better to feast on the turtle rather than to go hungry.

The turtle's three friends became much worried to see their friend trapped by the hunter. They sat together to think of some plan to free their friend from the hunter's snare. The crow then flew high up in the sky and spotted the hunter walking along the river bank. As per the plan the deer ran ahead of the hunter unnoticed and lay on the hunter's path as if dead.

The hunter saw the deer from a distance, lying on the ground. He was very happy to have found it again. "Now I'll have a good feast on it and sell its beautiful skin in the market," thought the hunter to himself. He put down the turtle onto the ground and ran to pick up the deer. In the meantime, as planned, the rat gnawed through the net and freed the turtle. The turtle hurriedly crawled away into the river water.

Unaware of the plot of these friends, the hunter went to fetch the dear for its tasty flesh and beautiful skin. But, what he saw with his mouth agape was that, when he reached near, the deer suddenly sprang up to its feet and darted away in the jungle. Before he could understand anything, the deer had disappeared.

Dejected, the hunter turned back to collect the turtle he had left behind on the ground in the snare. But he was shocked to see the snare lying nibbled at and the turtle missing. For a moment, the hunter thought that he was dreaming. But the damaged snare lying on the ground was proof enough to confirm that he was very much awake and he was compelled to believe that some miracle had taken place. The hunter got frightened on account of these happenings and ran out of the jungle.

The four friends once again started living happily.

Moral: - *A friend in need, is a friend indeed.*

CHAPTER 3

THE JACKAL AND THE DRUM

There was once a jackal named Gomaya who was staying in a jungle. Once he set out in search of food and ended up at an abandoned battlefield from where he heard loud and strange sounds. Though scared, jackal decided to know the secret of these sounds.

Carefully, the jackal marched in the direction of the sounds and found a drum there. It was this drum, which was sending the sounds whenever the branches of the tree above brushed against it.

Relieved, the jackal began playing the drum and thought that there could be food inside it. The jackal entered the drum by piercing its side. He was disappointed to find no food in it. Yet he consoled himself saying that he rid himself of the fear of sound.

Moral: - *Don't be afraid of false things.*

CHAPTER 4

THE MONGOOSE AND THE BABY

Once upon a time, there lived a poor Brahmin with his wife in a small village. The Brahmin used to perform Puja in religious functions taking place in nearby villages. They had no children. They offered prayers to god for a child. At last, a son was born to them.

The Brahmin's wife had a mongoose as her pet. The mongoose was very playful. It used to guard the Brahmin's house and also protect the baby, when he slept in the cradle.

Once, some people came to invite the Brahmin for performing Puja in their house. The Brahmin was in a dilemma. Should he go to perform Puja or stay home to look after his baby? His wife had also gone to fetch water from the well situated on the outskirts of the village.

The Brahmin didn't want to leave the baby all alone in the house, even though the mongoose was sitting there beside the cradle like a baby sitter. He was in a state of confusion.

But at last he buckled under the pressure and went to the nearby village to conduct the religious ceremony, leaving the baby all alone in the house.

The mongoose still sat beside the cradle guarding the baby. Suddenly, he saw a big snake crawling towards the cradle. Being a natural enemy of snakes and also having the responsibility of guarding the baby, he pounced upon the snake. After a fierce fighting with the snake, the mongoose killed it.

But the mouth and paws of the mongoose were smeared with the snake's blood. The mongoose was happy that he had done his duty faithfully and had saved the baby from the snake. He ran to the main entrance of the house and sat there waiting for his master's wife to come back. He thought that she would be highly impressed with his performance and shall reward him suitably.

After some time, the Brahmin's wife came along with the water pitcher on her head. She saw the paws and the mouth of the mongoose smeared in blood. She thought that the mongoose had killed her baby. In a fit of rage, she threw the heavy water pitcher on the head of the mongoose. The mongoose died on the spot.

The Brahmin's wife now went running inside the house. There she saw a big snake lying dead. The baby was sleeping safe in the cradle. Now she realized that she was greatly mistaken, and the mongoose had, in fact, saved her child. She began repenting and weeping. She had killed her faithful pet without knowing what had really happened.

***Moral**: - One should avoid taking hasty decisions in sensitive matters.*

CHAPTER 5

THE TALKATIVE TORTOISE

Once upon a time, two geese by the names of Sankata and Vikata and a tortoise by the name of Kambugriva lived near a river. They were good friends. Once, due to drought in the region, all the rivers, lakes and ponds went dry. There was not a drop of water to drink for the birds and animals. They began to die of thirst.

The three friends talked among themselves to find a solution to this problem and go out in search of water. But despite their best efforts they could not find water anywhere around. Having no alternative, the three friends decided to go to some distant lake, full of water, to settle down there forever. But there was a problem in shifting to so distant a place. While it was easy for the geese to fly, it was difficult for the tortoise to cover that distance on foot.

So the tortoise thought of a bright idea. He said, "Why not bring a strong stick? I will hold the stick in the middle with my teeth and you two hold both the ends of the stick in your beaks. In this manner, I can also travel with you."

Hearing the suggestion of the tortoise, the geese cautioned him, "It's a very good idea. We will do as you say. But you will have to be very careful. The problem with you is that you are very talkative. And if you open your mouth to say something while we are flying, it will definitely prove to be dangerous to you. So, don't talk while you are dangling by the stick, otherwise you will lose your hold and go crashing down on the ground and die."

The tortoise understood and promised not to open his mouth during the entire journey. So the geese held the stick ends in their beaks and the tortoise held the stick in the middle with his teeth and thus, they began their long journey.

They flew over hills, valleys, villages, forests and finally came over a town. While they were flying over the town, men, women and children came out of their houses to see this strange sight. The children began shouting and clapping. The foolish tortoise forgot that he was hanging precariously. He became so curious to know the reason behind these clapping that he opened his mouth to ask his friends-"Friends, what is this all about?" But as soon as he opened his mouth to utter these words, he loosened his hold on the stick and fell down on the ground and died instantaneously.

Moral: - *Always listen to friendly advice.*

CHAPTER 6

UNITED WE STAND

In the middle of the jungle there stood a big tree. A pair of sparrows lived on one of its branches. They had built a strong and comfortable nest and had two beautiful nestlings. They roamed the whole day in the jungle, collecting food to feed their young ones in the evening.

One day a huge elephant came to take rest under that big tree. He was hungry. So he tore off the branch on which the sparrows had built their nest. The branch fell onto the ground and the young ones of the birds were killed.

When the sparrows returned home in the evening, they found their young ones dead. They saw a big elephant lying under the tree and taking rest. Everything became crystal clear now. The elephant was the cause of the death of their loved young ones. The mother sparrow was grief-stricken. She began wailing over the loss of her nestlings.

Seeing her weeping bitterly, a woodpecker, who lived in a nearby tree, came to her to know the reason of her sorrow. The sparrows narrated the whole story. They expressed their wish to take revenge upon the elephant, for his cruel act. They wanted to see him dead.

"You're right", said the woodpecker. "This elephant has no consideration for others. He might, one day, kill my young ones too. Come with me. There is a sweet honey bee around here who's my friend. She is very intelligent. She might be able to tell us how the cruel elephant can be killed."

Having decided upon this, they went to meet the sweet honey bee. They narrated the whole story to her and expressed their wish. The bee consoled them and said, "Don't worry. I've a plan to kill that elephant.Listen, first I'll go to the elephant and sing a song in his ears. The elephant will close his eyes to listen attentively to my melody and when I have hummed him to sleep, the Woodpecker would poke his long beak into the elephant's eyes. This will turn him blind. Once he is blinded our job will be easy. I will go and express my sympathies and tell him to pour a few drops of the extract of a particular plant in his eyes to cure them. The elephant will go to fetch that plant. There will be a huge pit full of water lying in his way to the plant. When the elephant goes to collect the plant he will fall into the pit. Since, he will not be able to come out of it, he will die.

Then, as planned, the honey bee sang a song into the ears of the elephant. The elephant closed his eyes to listen to the melody more intently, and the woodpecker, without losing a single moment, made him blind by pecking at his eyes.

The cruel elephant shrieked with pain. He began crying- 'Oh, I have lost my eyes. I cannot see anything. Is there anyone who can help me?'

Immediately, the honey bee again flew to the elephant, who on the advice of the bee set out to fetch the miraculous plant. But on the way the blind elephant fell into the pit and died.

Thus, the sparrows avenged the untimely death of their young ones and by killing the cruel and foolish elephant, they saved many more lives of innocent creatures.

Moral: - *United we stand: Divided we fall.*

CHAPTER 7

THE CAMEL WITH A BELL

Once upon a time, a cart-maker and his family were traveling through a jungle, they saw a female camel suffering from labour pains. Seeing the female camel whining in pain, the cart-maker's wife pleaded with him to detain their journey for some time so that the poor animal could be rendered some help at this vital hour. The cart-maker's family stopped there and his wife began nursing the female camel. Soon, she gave birth to a baby camel.The cart-maker and his wife took great care of her and brought her to his house along with her baby. Gradually the baby camel grew to full size. Fondly, the cart-maker tied a bell round the neck of the young camel. Now whenever, the young camel would move around, the bell would jingle.

The cart-maker would sell the milk of the female camel and earn a lot of money, soon he purchased one more female camel. The fortune smiled on the cart-maker and soon he became the owner of a number of camels. All the camels used to go together to graze in a nearby jungle. The young camel was in a habit of trailing behind other camels. This was of great concern to other camels. They advised the young camel not to stray behind. But the young camel didn't pay heed to their advice.

One day, the camels were grazing in a nearby jungle. A lion heard the jingling of the bells. He followed the sound and saw a caravan of young camels grazing. He noticed one camel with a bell round his neck, strayed behind and still eating grass. The other camels assuaged their hunger and went back home. The young camel began to loiter around. The lion in the meantime, hid himself behind a bush. When the camel with the jingling bells came grazing near the bush the lion pounced upon him, killed and ate him.

Moral: - *Take heed of a good advice.*

CHAPTER 8

THE CUNNING JUDGE

Once Upon a time, there lived a sparrow in a tree. He was very happy to have a beautiful and comfortable nest of his own in the tree. The sparrow used to fly to far off places to pick the grains from so many fields, full of crops. By the sun set, he would return to his perch.

One day, the sparrow fly to pick grains, but could not return to his nest, because the heavy rains which continued for the whole night. The sparrow had to spend the whole night in a big banyan tree a little distance away from home.

The next morning, when the rain stopped and the sky became clear, the sparrow returned to his tree. He was astonished to find, "a rabbit occupying his beautiful and comfortable nest". The sparrow lost his temper and spoke to the rabbit, "It's my home you're sitting in. Please quit this place at once."

"Don't talk like fools," replied the rabbit. "Trees, rivers and lakes don't belong to anyone. Places like these are yours only so long as you are living in. If someone else occupies it in your absence, it belongs to the new occupant. So go away and don't disturb me anymore."

But the sparrow was not satisfied with this illogical reply He said, Let's ask a person of wisdom and only then our case will be settled. At a distance from the tree, there lived a wild cat. The cat, somehow, overheard the discussion that took place between the sparrow and the rabbit.

The cat immediately thought of a plan, took a holy dip in the river, and then sat like a priest and began chanting god's name in a loud tone. When the rabbit and the sparrow heard the cat chanting God's name, they approached him with a hope to get impartial justice and requested him to pass a judgement in the matter.

The cat became very happy to have both of them in front of him. He pretended to listen to their arguments. But as soon as the right opportunity came, the cat pounced upon both of them and killed and ate them together with great relish.

Moral: - *Fight over small matters might sometimes lead to a certain disaster.*

CHAPTER 9

THE MERCHANT'S SON

Long, long ago, there lived a merchant by the name of Sagaradatta, he had a son. The son once bought a book of poems. He recited a line of the poem so many times that he came to be known as, 'You get what you are destined to.' The father flew into a rage and said, "You are a fool. You can never come up in life. Leave my house at once. It has no place for you."

One day, a beautiful princess by the name of Chandrawati went to a festival in the city. There the princess saw a handsome prince and fell in love with him. Not being able to check her emotions, she said to her maid servant, "Find some way for me to meet this prince."

The maid met the prince and gave him the message of the princess. The prince agreed to meet the princess. He asked, "But where and how do I meet the princess?"

"Well," said the maid, "when it's dark you come to the white palace. There, you'll find a rope hanging from one of its windows. Climb up this rope to reach the princess' room."But on the appointed day, the prince backed out. He didn't turn up.

Meanwhile, 'you get what you are destined to' came wandering near the white palace. He saw a rope hanging there from one of its windows. He climbed up the rope and entered the room of the princess. As it was dark, the princess could not see the face of 'you get what you are destined to.' She thought that it was the same prince with whom she had fallen in love. She entertained him lavishly and talked to him for a long time, but the so called prince kept mum for all the while.

"Why don't you speak?" asked the princess.

"You always get what you are destined to," answered the merchant's son.

Hearing this the princess took a closer look at the merchant's son and soon realized that she was all through talking to a wrong man. She became furious and turned him out of her chamber.

Then 'you get what you are destined to', went to a nearby temple and slept there. The watchman of the temple had an appointment with someone in the same temple. So he requested the merchant's son to go and sleep in his quarter, which was situated at the rear side of the temple.

'You get what you are destined to,' instead, entered a wrong room. There the watchman's daughter Vinayavati was waiting for her lover. As it was pitch dark, she could not recognize the merchant's son and married him in the room itself according to Gandharva rites. Then she said," Why don't you talk to me?"

"You get what you are destined to," replied the merchant's son.

Vinayawati soon realized that she had been talking to a wrong man. So, she kicked out the merchant's son out of her house.

When he came out, he joined a passing marriage procession. The name of the bridegroom was Varakeerti.

When the marriage ceremony was about to start, a mad elephant, who'd already killed its master, appeared on the scene. Every one ran to safety.

Then 'you get what you are destined to' rushed to the brides help. He drove the elephant out by jabbing a long nail into its head. When the bridegroom returned and saw 'you get what you are destined to' holding his 'would-be' bride's hands he became angry. But the girl said that since 'you get what you are destined to' had saved her life from the mad elephant, she would marry him only.

And this girl was the same princess who had mistaken 'you get what you are destined to' for the prince, whom she had been waiting for in her room in the palace and after coming to know the truth, had kicked him out. The king also came to know of his daughter's decision.

Then, the king with great pomp and show married the princess with 'you get what you are destined to' and both of them lived happily, thereafter. So, at last, he really got what he was destined to.

Moral: - *Destiny plays an important role in life.*

CHAPTER 10

WHY THE OWLS BECAME ENEMIES OF THE CROWS

Long, long ago, all the birds of a jungle gathered to choose a new bird as their king. They were not happy with their king the Garuda, who they thought always enjoyed his time in the heaven and never cared for the birds. So, they thought it was better to choose a new bird as their king. A heated discussion followed in the meeting and ultimately it was decided to make the owl the king of birds. The birds started making preparation for the coronation of the newly elected king.

Just then a crow flew in and raised an objection in the meeting. He said laughing, "What a bird you've chosen as your king. An ugly fellow. He also goes blind during the day. Moreover, owls are birds of prey. He might kill other birds for his meals rather than save them. Didn't peacocks and swans suit as your king?".

The crow's arguments made the birds think over their decision again. It was decided to choose the king on some other occasion and hence the coronation ceremony was postponed.

The owl chosen as the king of birds, still waited for his coronation as king. He realized all of a sudden that there was absolute quiet around him. No one was talking, nothing was happening. Since, it is day time, he couldn't see anything around him. He grew very impatient and a little suspicious also. At last, overcome by his curiosity and eagerness for his coronation as king, he inquired from one of his attendants, the reason behind the delay.

The attendant said, "Sir, The coronation ceremony has been postponed. All the birds have decided to choose a new king, now not even a single bird is here. They have all gone back to their respective places."

The 'would be' king owl further lost his temper and said to the smiling crow who was still present there, "You've deprived me of the honor of becoming a king. So, from now on, we are sworn enemies of each other. Beware of us." The crow realized his folly, but it was too late now.

Moral: - *Think twice before you do or say anything.*

CHAPTER 11

THE VISIT OF THE SWAN

Once there lived a swan by the side of a big lake. The lake was situated in the middle of a dense forest. The swan was passing his days happily. One day, an owl came there. He drank the water of the lake and started living there."This is an isolated place," said the swan to the owl. "Besides, the lake goes dry during the summer season. It is better that you go to some other place to live in."

But the owl stayed on there saying that he loved calm and quiet places. Moreover, he liked the company of the swan.

"All right," replied the swan. "I too like your company. At least, there will be someone to talk to." So, the owl lived happily in his company for months together. But, when the summer arrived in all its vigor and the lake really went dry in due course, the owl thought of returning home. He thanked the swan for the nice company given by him and said with a heavy heart, "Dear friend, I am leaving this place now, since the lake has gone dry and there is no water available here.

I would like you to to come along with me, because you too can't live without water. "Thanks," said the swan, "in fact there is a small river that flows half a mile away from here, i shall go and stay there. When the river also goes dry, I shall come and join you and once again we will be enjoying each other's loving company." "All right," said the owl, "there is a big river, a few miles away from here. And on its bank there is a big banyan tree; I live in it."

And then, once again, thanking the swan for his nice company and hospitality, the owl flew away.

The swan shifted to the small river and began living there.After many days, when the small river also went dry and the swan felt lonely, he decided to meet the owl. One evening the swan flew and reached the banyan tree, the home of the owl. The owl was glad to receive the swan. He served tasty food and fresh water to his honored guest.

The swan was tired because of his long journey. He took his meals and went to sleep early. The owl perched itself on the same branch, a little away from where the swan slept.

Just then a few travelers came to rest under the tree. The sun had set. It was near dark all around. The half moon shone in the sky. Seeing the travelers the owl hooted sharply. The travelers took it as a bad omen. One of the travelers shot an arrow at the owl. As the owl could see in the dark, he ducked the arrow and flew away.

The arrow, instead, pierced the swan who was fast asleep at that time. The swan dropped dead on the ground.

Moral :- *Make friends among people who are like you.*

CHAPTER 12

A POOR BRAHMIN'S DREAM

Once upon a time, there lived a poor Brahmin in a village. His name was Swabhavakripna. He was all alone in this world. He had no relatives or friends. He used to beg for his living. Whatever food he got as alms, he kept in an earthen pot and hung it beside his bed. Whenever he felt hungry he took out some food from the pot and ate it.

One night, the Brahmin lay on his bed and soon he was fast asleep. He began to dream as he is no longer a poor Brahmin. He wore good clothes. He was the owner of a shop. Hundreds of customers came to his shop. Soon he became richer than before. He purchased many buffaloes and cows. Very soon the buffaloes and cows had their young ones. Those young ones grew and became buffaloes and cows. The buffaloes and cows gave milk. He made a lot of butter and curd from the milk. He sold butter and curd in the market. Soon he became richer than ever before. He built a big house for himself. Then he married a beautiful girl. Soon they had their children. The children played around all day making noise. He then scolded them and asked them to keep quiet. But they won't listen. So he picked up a stick and ran after them.

The Brahmin began to move his legs rapidly while he was still asleep. In doing so, he hit the earthen pot with one of his legs which was full of food. The pot broke and the food contents were spilled all over the foor.

The Brahmin woke up. He saw that he was still in the bed. All the edible items kept in the pot were scattered on the ground and became unfit for eating. All this happened because of his daydreaming.

Moral:- *One should not build castles in the air.*

CHAPTER 13

THE BULL AND THE LION

Once upon a time, a village merchant named Vardhmanaka, was going to Mathura town on his bullock cart. Two bullocks, Sanjeevaka and Nandaka were pulling the bullock cart.

While the merchant's cart was moving along the bank of the river Yamuna, Sanjeevaka, all of a sudden, stepped into a swampy spot. He tried to come out of the swamp, but couldn't succeed. The merchant too tried his level best to pull out Sanjeevaka from the swamp, but to no avail. Ultimately he had to leave Sanjeevaka there and proceed on with his onward journey.

Sanjeevaka thought sadly, "How I have served my master so loyally throughout my life and how my master has repaid my loyalty."

Now, Sanjeevaka was left to his fate. The only alternative he had to either resign to fate and die in the swamp or fight till the end. Sanjeevaka gathered up courage. He began applying his enormous muscle power. There is a saying- 'God helps those who help themselves.' At last after great effort, he managed to wriggle his way out of the swamp.

Now, as he had nowhere to go and he didn't want to return to his master's house, he started moving along the banks of the river. He ate green grass in the nearby forest and drank fresh water from the river. Soon he became healthy and stout. He started bellowing like a lion. His thunder like bellowing could be heard miles away.

Once, king lion whose name was Pingalaka, came to the river to drink water. Suddenly, he heard thunder-like bellowing. He got frightened and ran away into his cave.

King lion had two jackals named Damnaka and Kartaka as his ministers. When Damnaka came to know that some kind of fear had overpowered his king, he asked him, "Your Majesty, tell me who is he you are afraid of? I'll bring him to you."

The lion, being the king was not ready to admit the fact, but after great hesitation, he told Damnaka the real cause of his fear. Damnaka assured king lion that he will find out the actual source of the thundering sound.

Soon Damnaka brought Sanjeevaka to the court of his king. "Your Majesty, this is the animal, who has been making the thundering sound. He says that Lord Shiva has sent him to roam about in our kingdom." King lion was very pleased to talk to Sanjeevaka. Soon he became friendly with him. He spent much of his time chatting with Sanjeevaka. Gradually, king lion became very spiritual. He stopped killing his preys and even neglected his kingdom. This worried Damnaka and Kartaka and the other animals of the jungle.

Damnaka thought of a plan to solve the problem. One day, he went to king lion and said, "Your Majesty, Sanjeevaka has an evil eye on your kingdom. He wants to kill you and become the king himself."

And the next day, Damnaka went to Sanjeevaka and told him a different story. "King lion has a plan to kill you and distribute your flesh to all other animals of the jungle. Better you kill king lion with your pointed horns, before he kills you."

Sanjeevakaka became very angry to hear Damnaka's words. He went to the court of king lion and started bellowing in a thundering tone. This annoyed king lion and he pounced upon Sanjeevaka with a thundering roar.

Both were strong. With the result they engaged themselves in a fierce fight. Sanjeevaka tried to kill king lion with his pointed horns, but in vain. King lion killed Sanjeevaka with his sharp claws.

Though king lion killed Sanjeevaka but he felt very sad about it. After all, Sanjeevaka was once his friend. But since, Damnaka had convinced king lion that Sanjeevaka was a traitor, he had to act upon his advice. Later, he made Damnaka the chief minister of his kingdom.

Moral: - *Never befriend a natural enemy.*

CHAPTER 14

THE SAGE AND THE MOUSE

There lived a famous sage in a dense forest. Every day, the animals of the forest came to him to listen to his spiritual preachings. They would gather around the meditating sage and the sage would tell them the good things of life. There was also a little mouse living in the same forest. He too used to go to the sage daily to listen to his preachings.

One day, while he was roaming in the forest to collect berries for the sage, he was attacked by a big cat, who was watching him from behind the thick bushes.

The mouse was scared. He ran straight to the ashram of the sage. There he lay prostrate before the sage and narrated to him the whole story in a trembling voice. In the meantime, the cat also arrived there and requested the sage to allow him to take his prey.

The sage was in a fix. He thought for a moment and then with his divine powers transformed the mouse into a bigger cat. Seeing a huge cat before him the other cat ran away.

Now the mouse was carefree. He began to roam about in the forest like a big cat. He meowed loudly to frighten other animals. He fought with other cats to take revenge on them and in this way killed many of them.

The mouse had hardly enjoyed a few carefree days of his life, when one day, a fox pounced upon him. This was a new problem. He had never taken into account that there were yet bigger animals who could easily maul him and tear him into pieces. He ran for his life. He, somehow, saved himself from the fox and ran straight to the sage for help. The fox too was in his hot pursuit. Soon both of them stood before the sage.

The sage seeing the plight of the mouse this time, transformed the mouse into a bigger fox. Seeing a big fox before him the other fox ran away.

The mouse became more carefree and began roaming about in the forest more freely with his newly acquired status of a big fox. But, his happiness was short-lived.

One day, while he was moving around in the forest freely, a lion pounced upon him. The mouse, somehow, managed to save his life and as usual ran to take shelter in the ashram of the sage.

The sage, once again, took pity on the mouse and transformed him into a lion.

Now, the mouse, after acquiring the status of a lion, roamed fearlessly in the forest. He killed many animals in the forest unnecessarily. After having been transformed into a lion, the mouse had become all-powerful for the forest animals. He behaved like a king and commanded his subjects. But one thing always bothered his mind and kept him worried; and that was, the divine powers of the sage. "What, if, one day for some reason or the other, the sage becomes angry with me and brings me back to my original status," he would think worriedly. Ultimately, he decided something and one day, he came to the sage roaring loudly. He said to the sage, "I'm hungry. I want to eat you, so that I could enjoy all those divine powers, which you do. Allow me to kill you."

Hearing these words the sage became very angry. Sensing lion's evil designs, he immediately transformed the lion back into the mouse.

The worst had happened. Now the mouse realized his folly. He apologized to the saint for his evil actions and requested him to change him again into a lion. But the sage drove the mouse away by beating him with a stick.

Moral :- *However great one may become, one should never forget one's roots.*

CHAPTER 15

BEWARE OF MEAN FRIENDS

There in a deep jungle, lived a lion by the name of Madotkata. He had three selfish friends: a jackal, a crow and a leopard. They had become friendly with the lion, because he was the king of the forest. They were always at the service of the lion and obeyed him to meet their selfish ends.

Once, a camel got disorientated in the jungle while grazing and went astray. He tried hard to find his way out, but could not succeed.In the meantime, these three friends of the lion saw the camel, wandering in a confused manner.

"He doesn't seem to come from our forest", said the jackal to his friends. "Let's kill and eat him."

"No", said the leopard "It's a big animal. Let's go and inform our king, the lion."

"Yes, this is a good idea", said the crow. "We can have our share of flesh after the king kills the came."

Having decided upon this the three went to meet the lion.

"Your Majesty", said the jackal, "a camel from some other forest has entered into your kingdom without your permission. His body is full of delicious flesh. He may prove to be our best meal. Let's kill him".

Hearing the advice of his friends, the lion roared in anger and said, "What're you talking about? The camel has walked into my kingdom for the sake of his safety. We should give him shelter and not kill him. Go and bring him to me."

The three became very disheartened to hear the lion's words. But they were helpless. So having no alternative, they went to the camel and told him about the wishes of the lion who wanted to meet him and have dinner with him. The camel was terribly frightened to learn the awkward proposal. Thinking that his last moment had arrived and soon he would be killed by the king of the forest, he resigned himself to the mercy of his fate and went to see the lion in his den. However, the lion was very happy to see him. He talked to him sweetly and assured him of all the safety in the forest, so long as he stayed there. The camel was simply astonished and was very happy to hear the lion's words. He began living with the jackal, the wolf and the crow.

But once, bad luck struck the lion. One day, while he was hunting for food with his friends, he had a fight with a huge elephant. The fight was so fierce that all his three friends fled the spot in panic. The lion was' badly wounded in the fight. Although, he killed the elephant, but he himself became incapable of hunting for his food. Day after day, he had to go without food. His friends too had to starve for days together as they depended entirely on the lion's prey for their food. But the camel grazed around happily.

One day the three friends-the jackal, the leopard and the crow approached the lion and said, "Your Majesty, you're becoming weak day after day. We can't see you in this pitiable condition. Why don't you kill the camel and eat him?"

"No", roared the lion, "he is our guest. We can't kill him. Don't make such suggestions to me in future."

But the jackal, the leopard and the crow had set their evil eyes on the camel. They met together once again and hatched a plan to kill the camel.

They went to the camel and said, "My dear friend, you know our king has had nothing to eat for the last so many days. He cannot go hunting due to his wounds and physical infirmity. Under these circumstances, it becomes our duty to sacrifice ourselves to save the life of our king. Come, let us go to our king and offer our bodies for his food."

Innocent camel didn't understand their plot. He nodded and consented in favor of their proposal. All the four reached the den of the lion. The jackal said to the lion, "Your Majesty, despite our best of efforts, we couldn't find a prey."

First, the crow came forward and offered himself for the noble cause. "Sir, you can eat me and assuage your hunger", said the crow to the lion.

"Your body is too small", said the jackal. "How can the king assuage his hunger by eating you?"

The jackal offered his own body to the lion for food. He said, "Your Majesty, I offer myself. It's my solemn duty to save your life."

"No", said the leopard, "you too are too small to assuage the hunger of our King. I offer myself for this noble task. Kill me and eat me, Your Majesty," he said lying prostrate before the lion.

But the lion didn't kill any of them.

The camel was standing nearby and watching all that was going on there. He also decided to go forward and fulfill the formality. He stepped forward and said, "Your Majesty, why not me! You're my friend. A friend in need, is a friend indeed. Please kill me and eat my flesh to assuage your hunger."

The lion liked the camel's idea. Since, the camel himself had offered his body for food, his conscience won't prick and the jackal had already told the lion about the intense desire of the camel to sacrifice himself for the welfare of the king. He immediately pounced upon the camel and killed him. The lion and his friends had a good and sumptuous meal for days together.

Moral : - *Stay away from evil and mean people.*

CHAPTER 16

THE CLEVER HARE

There lived a lion by the name of Bhasuraka, in a dense jungle. He was very powerful, cruel and arrogant. He used to kill the animals of the jungle unnecessarily. He even killed the human beings, who travelled through the jungle. This became a cause of worry for all the animals. They discussed this problem among themselves and ultimately came upon a decision to hold a meeting with the lion and make an amicable settlement with him and put an end to this ongoing trauma.

So, one day, all the animals of the jungle assembled under a big tree. They also invited king lion to attend the meeting. In the meeting the animals said to king lion, "Your Majesty, we are happy that you are our king. We are more happy that you are presiding over the meeting." King lion thanked them and asked, "Why is it that we have gathered here?" All the animal began looking at each other. They had to muster enough courage to broach the topic. "Sir," said one of the animals, "It's natural that you kill us for food. But, killing more than what is required is a positive vice and unnecessary. If you go on killing the animals without any purpose, soon a day will come, when there will be no animals left in the jungle."

"So what do you want?" roared the king lion.

"Your Majesty, we have already discussed the problem among ourselves and have come upon a solution. We have decided to send one animal a day to your den. You can kill and eat it. This will save you from the trouble of hunting and you will not have to kill a number of animals unnecessarily for your meals."

"Good," the lion roared back. "I agree to this proposal, but the animals must reach to me in time, otherwise, I'll kill all the animals of the jungle." The animals agreed to this proposal.

Every day one animal walked into the lion's den to become his feast. The lion too was very happy to have his food right before him. He stopped hunting for his prey.

One day, it was the turn of a hare to go into the lion's den. The little hare was unwilling to go and become a meal of the lion, but the other animals forced him to go to the lion's den.

Having no alternative, the hare began thinking quickly. He thought of a plan. He began wandering around and made a deliberate delay, and reached the lion's den a little late than the lion's meal time. By now, the lion had already lost his patience and seeing the hare coming slowly, he became furious and demanded for an explanation.

"Your Majesty", the hare said with folded hands, "I am not to be blamed for that. I have come late because another lion began chasing me and wanted to eat me. He said that he too was the king of the jungle."

The king lion roared in great anger and said, "Impossible, there cannot exist another king in this jungle. Who is he? I'll kill him. Show me where he lives."

The lion and the hare set out to face the other lion. The hare took the lion to a deep well, full of water.

When they reached near the well, the hare said to the lion, "This is the place where he lives. He might be hiding inside."

The lion again roared in great anger, climbed up the well and peeped in. He saw his own reflection in the water and thought that the other lion was challenging his authority. He lost his temper.

"I must kill him", said the lion himself and jumped into the well. He was soon drowned.

The hare was happy. He went back to other animals and narrated the whole story. All the animals took a sigh of relief and praised him for his cleverness. They all lived happily thereafter.

Moral: - *Intelligence is superior to physical strength.*

CHAPTER 17

THE LOUSE AND THE BED-BUG

There lived a louse by the name of Mandarisarpini in the spacious bedroom of a mighty king. She used to live in the corner of the bed-sheet spread over the king's beautiful bedstead. Every day, when the king was fast asleep, the louse sipped his blood and crept back again into a corner of the bed-cover to hide herself.

One night, a bed-bug by the name of Agnimukha strolled into the bedroom of the king. The louse saw him and told him to get out since the whole of the bedroom was her territory only. But the bed-bug said to her cleverly,

"Look, you ought to be a little courteous to your guests. I'm your guest tonight." The louse got carried away by the bed-bug's sweet talks. She gave him shelter saying, "It's all right. You can stay here tonight. But, you will not bite the king to suck his blood."

"But I'm your guest. What will you give me to eat?" the clever bedbug asked. "What better food you can serve me than the king's blood."

"Well!", replied the louse. "You can suck the king's blood silently. He must not get hurt in any way."

"Agreed", said the clever bed-bug and waited for the king to arrive in the bedroom and sleep on the bed.

When the night fell, the king entered into his bedroom and slept on the bed.

The greedy bed-bug forgot all about his promises and bit the sleeping king hard to suck his blood.

"It's a royal blood", thought the bed-bug and continued sucking till the king felt a terrible itching in his skin. The king woke up and then ordered his servants to find the bed-bug and kill it.

But the bed-bug hid himself very cunningly into the joints of the bedstead and thus escaped his detection. The servants of the king, instead, found the louse on the bed-sheet. They caught her and killed her.

Moral: - *Never trust a stranger.*

CHAPTER 18

THE BLUE JACKAL

There lived a jackal in a jungle. His name was Chandarava. One day, he hadn't eaten anything since morning and was so hungry that he wandered and wandered across the jungle, but couldn't find anything to eat. He thought it better to walk a little further and find something to eat in some village. He reached a nearby small village. There on its outskirts he ate some food, but the quantity was not sufficient and he was still very hungry. Then he entered another village with the hope of getting some more food.

As soon as the jackal entered the village, a few dogs roaming there charged at him barking loudly. The jackal was terribly frightened. He began running through lanes in order to save himself from the dogs. Soon he saw a house. The door of the house was open. It was a washerman's house. 'This is the right place for me to hide', the jackal thought to himself and ran into the open door.

While trying to hide himself, the jackal slipped and fell into a tank full of blue color, which the washerman had kept ready to dye the clothes.

Soon the barking of the dogs ceased. The jackal saw them going away. He came out of the tub. There was a big mirror fixed on a wall of a room. There was no one around. The jackal entered the room and saw his image in the mirror. He was surprised to see his color. He looked blue. He came out of the house and ran back to the jungle.

When the animals of the jungle saw the blue jackal they were frightened. They had never seen such an animal. Even the lions and tigers were no exceptions. They too were scared of the seemingly strange animal.

The jackal was quick to realize the change in the behavior of the other animals. He decided to take advantage of this funny situation.

"Dear friends", said the blue jackal, "don't be afraid of me. I'm your well-wisher. Lord Brahma has sent me to look after your well-being. He has appointed me as your king."

All the animals of the jungle developed unshakable faith in the blue jackal and accepted him as their king. They brought presents for him and obeyed his commands. The blue jackal appointed the lion as his commander-in-chief; the wolf was appointed the defense minister and the elephant the home minister.

Thus, the blue jackal began living in luxury with the lions and tigers also at his command. What to talk of the smaller animals? The tigers and leopards brought him delicious food every day.

The blue jackal now was ruling the jungle. He used to hold daily court. All the animals were like his servants. Even the lion hunted small animals and gave them to the blue jackal to eat.

Once, when the blue jackal was holding his famous court, he heard a pack of jackals howling outside his palace. Those jackals had come from some other jungle and were howling, singing and dancing. The blue jackal forgot that he was a king and not an ordinary jackal any more. Instinctively, he too began howling, singing and dancing. All the animals were surprised to see their king howling like a jackal. Soon the word spread around that their king was simply a jackal and not a representative of Lord Brahma. He had fooled the animals. All the animals, in a fit of rage, killed the blue jackal immediately.

Moral: - *You cannot fool everyone all the time.*

CHAPTER 19

THE BIRD WITH TWO HEADS

Long, long ago, there lived a strange bird in a huge banyan tree. The tree stood beside a river. The strange bird had two heads, but only one stomach.

Once, while the bird was flying high in the sky, he saw an apple shaped fruit lying on the bank of the river. The bird swooped down, picked up the fruit and began to eat it. This was the most delicious fruit the bird had ever eaten. As the bird had two heads, the other head protested, "I'm your brother head. Why don't you let me also eat this tasty fruit?"

The first head of the bird replied, "Shut up. You know that we've only one stomach. Whichever head eats, the fruit will go to the same stomach. So it doesn't matter as to which head eats it. Moreover, I'm the one who found this fruit. So I've the first right to eat it."

Hearing this, the other head became silent. But this kind of selfishness on the part of the first head pinched him very much. One day, while flying, the other head spotted a tree bearing poisonous fruits. The other head immediately descended upon the tree and plucked a fruit from it.

"Please don't eat this poisonous fruit," cried the first head. "If you eat it, both of us will die, because we've a common stomach to digest it."

"Shut up!" shouted the other head. "Since I've plucked this fruit, I've every right to eat it."

The first head began to weep, but the other head didn't care. He wanted to take revenge. He ate the poisonous fruit. As a result both of them died.

Moral: - *People living in a family should never quarrel amongst themselves.*

CHAPTER 20

THE MUSICAL DONKEY

Once upon a time, there lived a washerman in a village. He had a donkey by the name of Udhata. He used to carry loads of clothes to the river bank and back home everyday.

The donkey was not satisfied with the food, that was given to him by his master to eat. So he wandered into the nearby fields stealthily and ate the crops growing there.

Once, the donkey, while wandering around, happened to meet a fox. Soon, both of them became friends and began to wander together in search of delicious food.

One night, the donkey and the fox were eating watermelons in a field. The watermelons were so tasty, that the donkey ate in a large quantity. Having eaten to his appetite, the donkey became so happy that he was compelled by an intense desire to sing. He told the fox that he was in such a good mood that he had to express his happiness in a melodious tone. "Don't be a fool. If you sing, the people sleeping in and around this field will wake up and beat us black and blue with sticks:' said the fox worriedly".

"You are a dull fellow", the donkey said hearing the words of the fox. "Singing makes one happy and healthy. No matter what comes, I'll definitely sing a song." The fox became worried to see the donkey adamant to sing a song in the midst of the field, while the owner was still sleeping only a little distance away.

Seeing his adamance, he said to the donkey, "Friend, wait a minute before you start. First, let me jump over to the other side of the fence for my safety." Saying so the fox jumped over to the other side of the fence without losing a moment.

The donkey began in his self-assumed melodious tone.

Hearing, suddenly, a donkey braying in the field, the owner woke up from his sleep. He picked up his stick lying by his side and ran towards the donkey who was still braying happily. The owner of the field looked around and saw the loss caused by the donkey. He became very angry and beat him and tied a heavy rock to his neck. The donkey, somehow, managed to drag himself out of the field with great difficulty.

The fox looked at the donkey and said in a sympathetic tone, "I'm sorry to see you in this pitiable condition. I had already warned you, but you didn't listen to my advice."The donkey too realized his folly and hung his head in shame.

Moral: - *Think before you act.*

CHAPTER 21

THE RABBITS AND THE ELEPHANTS

Once upon a time, there lived a herd of elephants in a deep jungle. Their king was a huge elephant by the name of Chaturdanta. In the middle of this jungle, there was a big lake where all the animals went to drink water. Once it so happened, that it didn't rain for the whole year and the lakes went dry. The elephants, after a great deal of discussion, decided to move to the other forest, where there was a lake named Chandrasar. This lake was full of water and never went dry even if there were no rains.

And so, the elephants set out for the lake 'Chandrasar'. They felt very happy upon reaching the new lake. They bathed in the fresh water of the lake and also enjoyed playing and spewing water on each other with their trunks. After having bathed satisfactorily and quenched their thirst with the sweet water of the lake they came out of it and entered the deep forest.

But, there lived many rabbits in their burrows around the lake area. When the herd of elephants walked around they stamped the burrows with their heavy feet. Thus, many rabbits were either killed or were left physically handicapped.

So, in order to salvage the grave situation, the rabbits held a meeting and discussed this new calamity. At one point, they decided to shift from that dangerous place and live somewhere else. But a rabbit named Lambkarna advised them to exercise patience. He offered his services for the sake of all the other rabbits and said, "Don't worry friends. Just see, how I drive these elephants away from this forest."

The next day, Lambkarna sat on a high rock. The rock lay in the main path of the elephants, leading to the lake. When the elephant passed by the rock, the rabbit addressed the king of the elephants in a tough voice, "You're a cruel fellow. You've trampled many of my relatives and friends under your feet. I too am king of rabbits. I stay in the heaven with God Moon. God Moon is very much annoyed with you."

The king elephant was frightened to hear this. He said in a trembling voice, "Please take me to God Moon. I'll ask for his forgiveness."

"All right", said the clever rabbit. "See me tonight at the lake." The king elephant, then, as told by the rabbit, reached the lake at night. The king rabbit and the king elephant both stood near the edge of the lake. It was a silent and moonlit night. Mild breeze was blowing. The rabbit asked the elephant to look carefully into the water of the lake. As soon as the king elephant looked into the lake, he saw the reflection of half moon in the lake's water. Just then a mild breeze blew and the reflection of the moon in the water became wavy.

Pointing to the wavy reflection of the moon, the king rabbit said,"Look for yourself, how annoyed God Moon is with you. Better you ask for his mercy, otherwise, he might curse you to death ". The king elephant became more and more frightened. He promised God Moon not to ever visit the lake with his friends.

The rabbits lived happily, thereafter.

Moral: - *Cleverness is strength.*

CHAPTER 22

THE BRAIN-LESS DONKEY

Once there lived a donkey in a town. The town was situated near a forest. There, in the forest lived king lion and his minister, a cunning fox. Once, king lion was badly wounded in a fierce fighting with an elephant. He became unable to hunt for his prey. So he asked his minister, the cunning fox to bring some good meal for him. As the fox used to share the prey, which king lion hunted for his meals, he at once, set out to search for food.

While wandering here and there, the fox met a donkey. The donkey looked foolish, nervous and hungry. The fox asked him, "Hello! You seem to be new to this forest. Where do you actually come from?"

"I come from the nearby town", said the donkey. "My master makes me work all day, but doesn't feed me properly. So I've left my home to find a better place to live in and eat properly."

"I see", said the fox. "Don't worry. I'm a senior minister in this forest kingdom. Come with me to the king's palace. Our king needs a bodyguard, who has the experience of town life. You will live in the palace and eat a lot of green grass growing around it"

The donkey was very happy to listen to all this from the minister fox of the forest kingdom. He proceeded with him to the royal palace.

Seeing a, donkey before him the king lion became highly impatient and pounced upon him immediately. But on account of constant hunger, the king lion had gone weak. He couldn't overpower the donkey. The donkey freed himself and ran for his life.

"Your Majesty," said the fox to king lion, "you shouldn't have acted in such a haste. You have scared your prey."

"I'm sorry," said king lion. "Try to bring him here once again."

The hungry fox went again to the donkey and said to him, "What a funny fellow you are. Why did you run away like that?"

"Why shouldn't I?' asked the donkey.

"My dear," said the fox, "you were being tested for your alertness as a royal bodyguard of the king. Thank God, you showed a quick reflex, otherwise, you would have been rejected for the job."

The donkey believed what the fox said and accompanied him once again to the palace. There at the palace the king lion was hiding behind the thick bushes. As soon as the donkey passed by the bushes, the lion pounced upon him and killed him instantly.

Just when the lion was about to begin eating the donkey, the fox said, "Your Majesty, you're going to have your meals after quite a few days. It's better you first take a bath and offer prayers."

"Hmm!" the king lion roared and said to the fox, "Stay here. I'll be back right now."

The lion went to take a bath and offer his prayers. In the meantime, the fox ate the donkey's brain. When the king lion came back to eat his prey, he was surprised to see that the donkey's brain was missing.

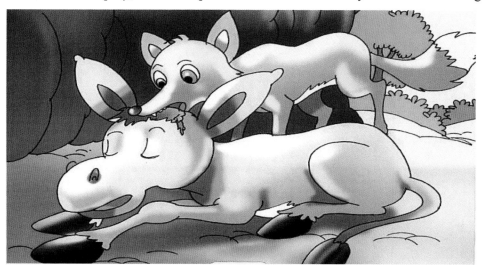

"Where is this donkey's brain?" The king lion roared in great anger.

"The donkey's brain!" the fox expressed his surprise. "Your Majesty, you're fully aware that donkeys don't have a brain. Had that donkey ever had a brain, he would never have come with me to this palace for the second time."

"Yes," agreed king lion, "that's the point. I agree that the donkeys do not have a brain"

Moral: - *Sometimes a cunning argument outwits normal intelligence.*

CHAPTER 23

THE MARRIAGE OF A SNAKE

There lived a Brahmin and his wife in a small village. The Brahmin couple had no children. They prayed day and night to God in order to be blessed with a child. After years of praying, their wishes materialized and they were blessed with a child. But to everybody's shock, the child was a snake and not a normal human baby. The Brahmin couple was advised by their friends and relatives to get rid of the snake, as quickly as possible. But the Brahmin's wife didn't listen to their suggestions and continued to look after the snake as her own baby.

Years passed by and the snake grew up bigger and bigger, till he reached the age of marriage. Now the Brahmin couple started looking for a suitable girl for their snake son. The Brahmin went from village to village and town to town in search of a suitable girl, but all in vain. "How can a human being marry our snake child?" said the Brahmin to his wife. But his wife insisted for a suitable match for her son.

Having lost all the hopes from all sides, the Brahmin approached one of his old friends. He narrated his problem to his friend. "Oh! You should've told me about it earlier," said his friend. "I'm myself looking for a suitable match for my daughter. I shall be too happy to give her in marriage with your snake son." The Brahmin couldn't believe his ears. But the marriage was solemnized despite protests. The girl was herself adamant to marry Brahmin's son, be it a snake, no matter.

After marriage the newly married couple the girl and the snake started to live like an ideal wife and husband. The girl looked after her husband's comforts dutifully. Her husband-the snake-slept beside his wife coiled in a basket.

One night, the snake crawled out of the basket into a room. After a few moments a young man came out of the room. He woke up the girl. The girl seeing a man in his room was about to scream when the young man said to her, "Don't be foolish. I'm your husband."

The girl didn't believe the young man. She said, "Show it to me before my eyes. I still don't believe it. " So the young man again slipped into the empty shell of the snake and then came out of it again transformed into a man. The girl became very happy to find such a husband. When the Brahmin and his wife came to know of this secret, they too became very happy.

One night, the Brahmin kept a watch over his son. As soon as his son came out of the snake's body transformed into a young man, the Brahmin got hold of the snake's empty outer covering and threw it into the fire.

Then his son came to him and said, "Father, you've saved my life. Now, I can never be transformed into a snake. My outer covering has been destroyed in fire and with it has ended the long curse upon me."

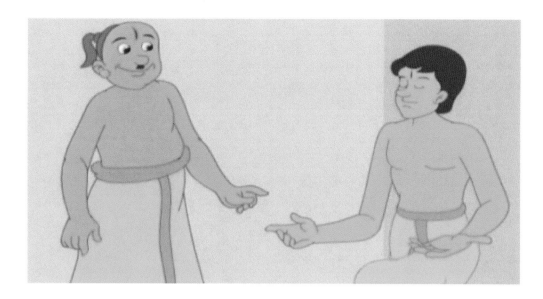

So the Brahmin, his wife, son and daughter-in-law, all began to live a happy life, thereafter. The villagers too were happy to see them leading a normal and healthy life.

Moral: - *After rains comes the sunshine.*

CHAPTER 24

THE TRICK OF THE CROW

Once upon a time, there stood a huge tree on the outskirts of a small village. In this, tree there lived a pair of crows with their young ones. And at the root of the tree there lived a big serpent in a deep hole. Every time the crows laid their eggs, the serpent crept up the tree and ate all the eggs and the young ones. With the result, the crows were never able to raise their young ones. This made the crows very sad. They didn't know how to get rid of the killer serpent.

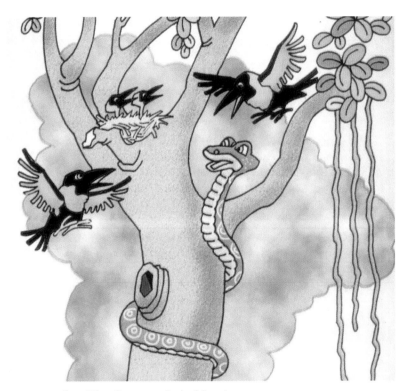

One day, the crows went to a fox. The fox was their friend.

"Hello dear friends, come in", said the fox seeing the crows at his door, "You two seem to be very sad. What's the matter?"

"The root cause of our problem is a bad serpent. He is after us. He eats up our eggs and the young ones. Please help us get rid of this serpent," said the female crow to the fox.

The fox too was shocked to hear this sad story. She promised to help the crows. She thought for a few minutes and then laid out a plan before the crows.

"Listen carefully", said the fox, "you know where the king's palace is situated. You've also seen the queen taking bath in an open swimming pool, inside the palace. The queen, while taking bath always removes all her ornaments and keeps them on a tray kept by the side of the pool. While she is busy taking her bath, you two swoop down upon the tray and pick up two diamond ornaments from it. Drop them into the serpent's hole. The servants of the queen will come chasing you and finding the ornaments into the serpent's hole, they will first kill the serpent to save them from being bitten by it and then will take the ornaments out of the hole. Thus, the serpent will be killed and you too will be saved from all the troubles of killing it by yourself."

This was a very bright idea. The crows liked it. They flew to the king's palace. There they saw the queen taking bath in a swimming pool. She had removed her ornaments and kept them in a tray.

The crows swooped down upon the tray, picked up two expensive diamond necklaces from it and flew towards the snake's hole. The guards ran after the crows brandishing their sticks and swords.

They chased the crows and soon reached that big tree, where the big snake lived. They found the diamond necklaces, lying inside the serpent's hole. Afraid of the snake, they first killed the snake by sticks and swords and then took out the ornaments and returned to the palace.

The crows thanked the fox for her help and lived happily in the tree, thereafter.

Moral: - *Intelligence is greater than physical strength.*

CHAPTER 25

THE CLEVER DOVES

There was a huge banyan tree standing on the outer boundaries of a village. All kinds of birds had their homes in this tree. Even the travelers would come and relax under its cool shade during the hot summer days.

Once, a fowler came to take a rest there. He also had a huge net with him. He set his net under the tree and strewed some grains of rice to lure the birds. A crow living in the tree saw it and cautioned his friends not to go down to eat the rice.

But at the same moment, a flock of doves came flying over the banyan tree. They saw grains of rice strewn around and without losing a moment, descended on the ground to eat the grains of rice. As soon as they started eating the rice, a huge net fell over them and they were all trapped. They tried everything to come out of the net, but in vain. They saw the fowler coming towards them. He was very happy to find a large number of doves trapped inside the net.

However, the king of doves was very intelligent and clever. He said to other doves, "We must do something immediately to free ourselves from the clutches of this fowler. I've an idea. We should all fly up together clutching the net in our beaks. We will decide our next course of action later. Now, come on friends, let's fly."

So each dove picked up a part of the huge net in his beak and they all flew up together. Seeing the birds flying along with the whole net, the fowler was surprised. He could never imagine this. He ran after the flying birds, shouting madly, but could not catch them. Soon the birds flew out of his sight.

When the king dove saw that the fowler had given up the chase, he said to his friends, "Now we all have to get out of this net. There lives a mouse on the nearby hillock. He is my friend. Let's go to him for his help."

All the doves flew on to meet the mouse. When the mouse heard the doves making noise in front of his hole, he got frightened and hid himself deeper into the hole. He came out only when he heard the king dove saying, "Friend, it's the king dove. We're in great difficulty. Please come out and help us."

Hearing the dove, his friend's voice, the mouse came out of his hole and saw the king dove and his friends trapped in the net.

"Oh!", said the mouse, "Who's done all this to you?"

The king dove narrated the whole story. The mouse immediately started nibbling at the net around the king dove. The king dove said, "No, my friend. First set my followers free. A king cannot keep his subjects in pain and enjoy the freedom for himself."

The mouse praised the king dove for his nobleness and nibbled at the portion of the net, which would set free the other doves first. And only at last, he freed the king dove.

All the doves were very grateful to the mouse. They thanked the mouse and then flew to their destination happily.

Moral : - *Unity is strength.*

CHAPTER 26

THE LIONESS AND THE YOUNG JACKAL

Long, long ago, there lived a lion couple in a dense forest. One day, the lioness gave birth to two cubs. Now the lion would go out hunting and bring home a prey for the lioness and the cubs.

However, one day, the lion wandered for a long time in search of food, but all in vain. Soon the sun set and the desperate lion decided to return home. While on his way back home, he came across a baby jackal. The lion taking pity on the baby jackal didn't kill it. Instead, he fetched it home safely and presented it to his wife.

"My dear", asked his wife, "What's it? Is it for my meals?"

"It's a baby jackal, which I found on my way back home. I didn't kill it, because it's simply a baby. However, it is up to you; if you wish, you can eat it."

"Since you didn't kill this baby yourself. I too spare its life. I shall look after this baby jackal as my own third son," said the lioness. Thus, the couple decided to rear the newcomer as their own baby. She also began to feed the baby jackal on her own milk. Soon the baby jackal became fat and healthy. The three babies grew up together without realizing any difference between them. The baby jackal played with the lion's cubs, as if it was one of them.

One day, while the three were playing outside their cave, they saw an elephant trumpeting near the cave. Despite the enormous size of the elephant the lion cubs became furious to see it and took an attacking posture instinctively Whereas, the young jackal shouted, "Hold it! Don't go near this huge animal. He is our enemy" Howling like this the young jackal ran back towards his home. For the first time, the cubs were face to face with cowardliness. This was not in their traits but since they were young and quite inexperienced, they were discouraged to see the baby jackal running away from the battle-field. The cubs also returned home gloomy and dejected. They went to their mother and narrated to her the story of their brother's cowardice.

The young jackal was irritated to see his brothers making complaints to their mother about him. He abused his brothers in great anger and shoved them about.

The lioness sank into deep thought and decided to reveal the truth of the origin of the baby jackal to him before it was too late and became dangerous for his life. She also felt that since it was time of the growth of the cubs, and development of their natural instincts and traits, the company of the cowardly baby jackal will only hamper the prospects of their growth. So, she said to him with deep concern, listen son, the truth is that you are the son of a jackal. Since you were an orphan, I took pity on you and reared you as my own child. You're no doubt, smart and intelligent, but no elephants are ever killed in the family you were born in. Better you return to your clan before our sons come to know this truth about you and kill you."

The young jackal was terrified to know this truth. He immediately fled from the cave, into the deep jungle to live with his own clan.

Moral: - *One should always be in one's own company.*

CHAPTER 27

THE MONKEY'S REVENGE

Once upon a time there lived a king by the name of Chandra. He had a beautiful palace surrounded by a huge garden. In this garden there lived many birds. Even monkeys had their homes in it. The king had also a goat for his sons to play with. The goat had long wool like hair on his body. Being a glutton he would enter into the royal kitchen and eat whatever food was stocked there. The chief cook didn't like this goat and would, sometimes, beat him with smoldering sticks to drive him out of the kitchen.

The chief of the monkeys had witnessed the scene many times. He was very intelligent. Seeing the hairy goat being thrashed with smoldering sticks almost every day, he thought to himself: "This hairy goat, despite being thrashed with smoldering sticks by the chief cook repeatedly, doesn't shun his habit. This may become very irritating for the cooks. One day the cooks might set the hairy goat on fire. The goat might rush into the stable with his wool like hair blazing and roll onto the hay in pain and panic. As a result the hay will catch fire. Thus many horses will get burnt. And it is said that the fat of a freshly killed monkey is applied to cure the burns of a horse. If such a situation ever arises, we monkeys are sure to be slaughtered."

The chief of the monkeys, then, advised his followers to abandon the palace garden, as early as possible, But the other monkeys didn't pay heed to his sincere advice. So the monkey chief decided to himself leave the palace garden and go to some other distant place, where he would be safe and secure. So he left for a distant jungle to live in there.

One day, shortly after the goat had entered the royal kitchen, a cook picked up a burning log and struck the goat with it. The goat's hair caught fire. The goat rushed into the stable with his hair blazing. He rolled over the heap of hay to extinguish the fire but instead, the hay caught fire. The flames leapt up to the roof of the stable. Many horses were burnt to death whereas a number of them received burn injuries. The king was shocked to learn that his horses had sustained burn injuries. He called the veterinary doctor for treatment of the animals. The doctor advised the king to bring monkey fat. He said, "Your Majesty, if the fat of a freshly killed monkey is applied to the burns of the horses, they would be cured."

The king immediately ordered for the killing of the monkeys. Soon thousands of monkeys were killed and their fat was applied to the burns of the horses. When the monkey-chief who was living in some other jungle came to know of this killing, he became very sad. He vowed to take revenge on the king.

Once the chief of monkeys went to a nearby lake to quench his thirst. There, his attention was diverted to some footprints which were all pointing towards the lake, but not a single one was pointing away from the lake. Just then, a big black giant came out of the lake's water, with a necklace of jewels round his neck. The chief of monkeys was frightened, but the black giant said, "I'm very happy with you. You were clever not to enter the lake. Whoever enters this lake is eaten by me. I can eat thousands of people at a time. I'm pleased with you. You may ask me for granting a boon to you. Please speak."

"So listen!" said the monkey chief, "I've great enmity with king Chandra. He ordered the slaughter of my brothers, for the purpose of using their fat to rub on the burnt skin of the horses."

"Bring the king and his men into this lake and I'll devour all of them," the black monster said to the monkey-chief.

"Please give me your jewel necklace," the monkey-chief said. "I'll bring you a lot of royal people for your meal."

The black giant happily gave the necklace to the monkey-chief.

The monkey-chief put the necklace round his neck and went to the king's palace. The chief of monkey told the king that there was a lake nearby and it was full of jewels. He said that he had brought one such necklace to show as sample. The king listened intently about the lake of jewels and asked the monkey-chief to tell more about it.

The monkey-chief said, "To get a jewel necklace, like the one I've, one has to take a bath in the lake before sunrise. So, please take all your men with you to the lake, Your Majesty."

The king became very happy with this invitation. The next morning he set out for the lake with his family members and hundreds of his courtiers. After arriving at the lake the monkey-chief said to the king,

"Your Majesty, wait here. Let others go into the lake first to take the necklace. Since you're a king, you'll be presented with a special necklace."

While the king waited near the lake, his family members and courtiers all jumped into the lake to collect the jeweled necklace.

The king waited for a long time for his family members to emerge out of the lake. But none of them came out. In the meantime, the monkey-chief climbed up a nearby tree. He said to the king, "You foolish king! Your family members and courtiers, all have been devoured by the black giant living in the lake. You killed my family and I've had my revenge on you. There is a saying; 'It's no sin to return evil for evil.' I saved you because once you were my master."

When the king heard this he became sad and returned to his kingdom crestfallen.

Moral:- *Tit for tat.*

CHAPTER 28

THE ROTATING WHEEL

Once upon a time, there were four Brahmin friends. Despite their learnings they were very poor. At last they got tired of their poverty and decided to go to another country to earn money. They reached Ujjayini. After taking their bath in the river Shipra they paid a visit to Mahakaleshwar temple. As they were coming out of the temple they met a hermit named Bhairawanad. They accompanied him to his hermitage.

After treating his guests, the hermit asked them - "Where have you come from and where do you want to go?" They replied - "We are poor Brahmins. We want to earn wealth. We have decided that either we will become wealthy or we will give up our lives." They also sought his help in this regard. Bhairwanad then gave them four lamps whose wicks were initiated with the powers of mantra. He said to them - "Go towards the Himalayas and walk until the wicks of your lamps begin to fall one by one. Digging at the place where the wicks of your lamp fall you will find wealth."

The four friends proceeded towards the Himalayas carrying the lamps in their hands. After some time, wick of one of the friend's lamp fell down. All of them dug up that place. They were amazed to find a copper-mine there. The first Brahmin told his friends to take all the copper, but they refused. So he took as much copper as he could carry and returned to his home.

Remaining three friends proceeded further. After traveling for some time, the wick of the second friend's lamp fell down. They dug up that place and found a silver-mine there. The second friend asked his friends to take all the silver but they refused to take it. They thought first it was a mine of copper, then it was a mine of silver. May be they strike the gold third time. The second friend took as much silver as he could carry and returned back.

Now only two friends were left. They proceeded further. The wick of the third friend's lamp fell down at a place. Both of them dug up that place and were amazed to find a mine of gold. He told the fourth friend to take all the gold but the fourth friend refused to take it because he was anticipating gems and jewels in his turn. The third friend took as much gold as he could carry and returned. The fourth friend requested him to come along with him, but the third refused and said -"I will wait for you at this place. You go and try your luck."

The fourth friend proceeded further alone. After walking for some distance he found an injured man lying on the ground and a wheel spinning over him. He went near that man and said - "Who are you? How did you get injured and why is this wheel spinning over your head?" Hardly the fourth friend finished his words, the wheel left the injured man and stuck to the head of the Brahmin.

The injured man replied that just like him, he too had come there in search of gold and found an injured man and asked him the same question and ..."since then the wheel has been spinning over my head. Now your miseries would only end when a man arrives here with a desire of wealth in his heart." saying this the injured man disappeared while the fourth friend remained there with the wheel spinning on his head.

Now, when the third friend found that his friend was taking too long to return, he set out to find him. He finally arrived at the same place, where his fourth friend was standing drenched in blood, with a wheel whirling over his head.

"What is this?" he asked his fourth friend in great astonishment.

"This is the result of my greed for wealth," replied the fourth friend and narrated the whole story, weeping and moaning.

"I'm sorry to see your ill-fate, friend. But you didn't listen to me, when I offered you gold. You wanted more. Now I can only wish you all the best," said the third friend and went away with a sad heart.

Moral: - *Greed is harmful.*

CHAPTER 29

THE PRINCE AND THE SEEDLING

Once there was a king whose son was very ill-tempered and bad mannered. The king, the courtiers and many other eminent citizens tried to reform the prince and make him understand the bad impression his ill manners and wicked ways would create on the public. But the prince paid no heed to their sensible advices.

One day a sage came to the king's court. He was received with great honor by the king and his courtiers. When the king came to know that the sage was trying to find out a good dwelling place for himself, he offered him a hermitage in his palace. The sage accepted the offer of the king and started living in the hermitage.

One day, the king said to the sage, "You would have probably come to know by now, that my son is very ill-tempered and bad mannered. The people of my kingdom call him an unworthy prince. They don't want him to succeed me as king. I request you kindly to teach the prince to mend his ways" Then the king discussed other matters of his kingdom with the sage and left his son under his direct care and guidance with a confidence that the sage will definitely ameliorate the prince and bring a positive reform in him.

The next day, the sage took the prince for a walk through the garden of the palace. Pointing to a tiny plant the sage said to the prince, "Eat a leaf of this plant and tell me how it tastes."

The moment the prince tasted the leaf he immediately spat it on the ground. "It seems to be a poisonous seedling. If it is allowed to grow into a big tree, it may prove dangerous for the health of many people." The prince pulled the tiny plant out of the ground and tore it to pieces.

Then the sage picked up the torn and mutilated plant and said to the prince, "As you've reacted in the case of this plant, the people of your kingdom may, one day, react in the same manner with you, because they think you are a wicked prince. They may not allow you to rule the kingdom and may send you to exile. So it is much better that you mend your ways to create a feeling of mercy, compassion and kind heartedness all around "

The prince understood the message of the sage. From that day onwards, he tried to grow humble and kind hearted, full of mercy and love. The king was pleased and extremely happy to see such a big change in his son. He thanked the sage and expressed his gratefulness for his kindness.

Moral: - *Bad temperament does not win hearts.*

CHAPTER 30

THE WEDDING OF THE MOUSE

Long ago, there lived a small female mouse near sage Salankayana's ashram. One day after being almost killed by a bird, she prayed Salankayana, "O sage, please give me shelter in your hermitage. Otherwise, some wicked bird will kill me. I will spend the rest of my life with whatever leftovers you choose to feed me with."

The female mouse's prayer moved the sage but he thought that if he took her home, people would laugh at him. So, he turned the mouse into a small girl and took her home.

"What is this you have brought," asked the sage's wife. Where did you bring this girl from?"

"She is a female mouse". She needed protection from wicked birds. That's why I turned her into a girl and brought her home.

"You will need to shower all care on her. I will make her a mouse again," said the sage.

"Please don't do that," pleaded his wife, "You have saved her life and therefore you have become her father. I don't have a child. Since you are her father, she becomes my daughter." The sage accepted her plea.

The girl grew into a beautiful woman and became an eligible bride. Salankayana told his wife, "The girl has come of age. It is not proper for her to remain in our house. The learned have said, He who keeps an eligible bride in his house forfeits a place in

Heaven. "So do his ancestors."

"It's all right. Look for a boy," said his wife.

Salankayana immediately summoned the Sun and told him, "This is my daughter. If she is willing to marry you, get ready to marry her."

He then showed the Sun to his daughter and asked her if she would marry him. She said that the Sun was very hot and she would prefer someone else. The sage then summoned the God of Clouds, the God of Wind and the God of Mountains. The girl rejected every one of them on one ground or the other.

Then the God of Mountains told the sage, "The most suitable candidate for your daughter is a mouse. He is more powerful than me."

The girl was very happy and she readily accepted to wed the mouse. The sage then turned her into a mouse and gave her away to a king of mice in marriage.

Moral: - *Ingrained traits are difficult to change.*

CHAPTER 31

HELLO! CAVE

Long ago, there lived a lion by the name of Kharanakhara. He had been trying to hunt for his prey for the last two days, but could not succeed due to his old age and physical infirmity. He was no longer strong to hunt for his food. He was quite dejected and disappointed. He thought that he would die of starving. One day, while he was wandering in the jungle hopelessly, he came across a cave. 'There must be some animal who lives in this cave'; so thought the lion. 'I will hide myself in it and wait for its occupant to enter. And as soon as the occupant enters the cave, I shall kill him and eat his flesh.' Thinking thus, the lion entered the cave and hid himself carefully.

After some time, a fox came near the cave. The cave belonged to her. The fox was surprised to find the foot-marks of a lion pointing towards the cave. 'Some lion stealthily entered my cave', she thought to herself. But to make sure of the presence of the lion inside the cave, the fox played upon a trick.

The fox stood at some distance from the cave to save herself in case of a sudden attack and shouted, "Hello cave! I've come back. Speak to me as you have been doing earlier. Why're you keeping silent, my dear cave? May I come in and occupy my residence?"

Hearing the fox calling the cave, the lion thought to himself, that the cave he was hiding in, must in reality be a talking cave. The cave might be keeping quiet because of his kingly presence inside. Therefore, if the cave didn't answer to the fox's question, the fox might go away to occupy some other cave and thus, he would have to go without a meal once again.

Trying to be wise, the lion answered in a roaring voice on behalf of the cave, "I've not forgotten my practice of speaking to you when you come, my dear fox. Come in and be at home, please."

Thus, the clever fox confirmed the presence of the lion hiding in her cave and ran away without losing a single moment, saying, "Only a fool would believe that a cave speaks."

Moral: - *Presence of mind is the best weapon to guard oneself.*

CHAPTER 32

THE OLD GREEDY CRANE

There was an old crane, who lived by a lake. He was so old that he could not arrange for his food. The fish swam around him, but he was so weak that he could not catch them.

One day, he was very hungry. He hadn't had anything to eat for days together. In total dejection he sat on the bank of the lake and began weeping. A crab who was passing by, heard him crying and asked him for the reason.

All of a sudden, he hit upon an idea. He asked the crab to have patience and allow him some time to overcome his emotion. The crab consoled him and became silent. Meanwhile, the crane pretended to have overcome his emotions and began saying in a sad tone, "Perhaps, you are not aware of the future of the aquatic animals of this lake. They will soon die without water."

"What!" the crab exclaimed.

"Yes", the crane said. "A fortune teller has told me that very soon this lake will go dry and all the creatures living in it will die. This thought of impending doom has sunken my heart with grief." After a pause, the crane continued, "There is another lake at some distance from here. All the big creatures like crocodiles, tortoises, frogs etc. can travel up to that lake. But I am worried about those, who cannot travel by land, like fish. They will die without water. This is the reason why I am so sad. I want to help them."

All the creatures in the lake were shocked to know the future of the lake but they became very happy to know that the crane was ready to help them.

"There is a big lake, full of water, a few miles away from here. I'll carry such helpless creatures on my back", said the crane, "and put them safely in the big lake."

Everyone on the lake agreed to this proposal. Now the crane has started carrying one creature at a time, on his back. First, he started with fish and carried them on his back; but, instead of taking them to the big lake, he took them to a nearby hill and ate them. And in this way, the crane ate a large number of fish everyday. Within a few days, he regained his health and became fat.

One day, the crab said to the crane, "Friend, you seem to have forgotten me. I thought, I would be the first one to be carried to the big lake, but I have a feeling that I have been completely ignored."

"No, I haven't forgotten you", said the crane cunningly. He was tired of eating fish everyday. He wanted to have a change. So he said to the crab, "Come my friend. Sit on my back"

The crab gladly sat on the crane's back and the crane flew towards the big lake. "How far is the lake now?" the crab asked. The crane thought that the crab was quite an innocent creature. He would never know his evil plans. So, he said angrily, "You fool, do you think I am your servant? There is no other lake around here. I made this plan in order to be able to eat you all. Now you too are prepared to die."

But the crab didn't loose his senses. He quickly grabbed the long neck of the crane with his sharp claws and told him to return to the old lake. He threatened to cut the crane's neck into two, if he didn't obey him.

The crane was left with no choice, but to return to the old lake. On reaching the lake the crab immediately jumped off the back of the crane. Then he told all the other creatures about the crane's misdeeds. This made the creatures very angry. They attacked the crane and killed him.

Moral: - *Never be greedy.*

CHAPTER 33

WOLF ! WOLF !!

There lived a shepherd in a village. He had many sheep. He took them out every morning for grazing. One day, his wife fell ill and he had to go to the city to purchase some medicines for his ailing wife. 'There will be no one to take care of the sheep', he thought to himself. Then he called his son and told him, " I'm going to the city to purchase some medicines for your mother. It will take me two or three days to come back. So take care of the sheep. Save them from being attacked by the tigers and wolves. There are many wild animals in the nearby forest. They might kill our sheep."

The boy listened to his father's advice carefully and the next day, he left for the nearby hillside with his flock of sheep. But he was a mischievous boy. He was feeling lonely. So he wanted to have some fun. He stood on a high rock and began shouting "Wolf! Wolf!, help."

The villagers heard the boy crying for help. They ran towards the hillside to help the boy, carrying big sticks in their hands. When they reached there they found that there was no wolf.

The sheep were grazing happily and the shepherd boy was playing on a flute.

"Where is the wolf?" the villagers asked the boy.

"There is no wolf here. I was joking," the boy said and laughed.

The villagers became very angry and returned to their work in the village.

Next day, the boy played the same trick. The villagers again reached there to help the boy. But when they came to know that the boy was lying, they felt highly annoyed and went back to the village cursing the boy.

But on the third day, a wolf really came there. The boy got frightened to see his red eyes. The wolf was huffing and growling. He began advancing towards the flock of sheep, gnashing his teeth and lolling his tongue. The boy lost his courage and began trembling with fear. He shouted, "Wolf, wolf, please help!" But to no avail.

This time no one came to help him. The villagers thought that the boy was up to his old tricks. The wolf killed many of his sheep. The boy returned home weeping.

Moral: - *People do not trust a liar.*

CHAPTER 34

THE KING COBRA AND THE ANTS

There lived a big king cobra in a dense forest. As usual, he fed on birds' eggs, lizards, frogs and other small creatures. The whole night he hunted the small creatures and when the day broke, he went into his hole to sleep in. Gradually, he became fat. And his fat grew to such a measure that it became difficult for him to enter and come out of his hole without being scratched.

Ultimately, he decided to abandon his hole and selected a huge tree for his new home. But there was an ant hill at the root of the tree. It was impossible for king cobra to put up with the ants. So, he went to the ant hill and said, "I'm King Cobra, the king of this forest. I order all of you to go from this place and live somewhere else."

There were other animals, too, around. They began trembling with fear to see such a huge snake before them. They ran for their lives. But the ants paid no heed to his threats. Thousands of ants streamed out of the ant hill. Soon they were swarming all over the body of the king cobra, stinging and biting him. Thousands of thorny pricks all over his body caused unbearable pain to him. The king cobra tried to keep the ants away, but in vain. He wriggled in pain and died at last.

Moral: - *Sometimes even a small person can be a formidable foe.*

CHAPTER 35

THE BEAR AND TWO FRIENDS

Golu amd Molu were fast friends. For a major period of the day, they would be seen together. Everyone admired their friendship. Once, they got an invitation from one of their friends, who had invited them to attend his sister's marriage. The marriage was to take place in a nearby village.

But in order to reach the village, one had to pass through a forest, which was full of wild animals like tigers and bears etc. While walking through the forest, Golu and Molu saw a bear coming towards them. Both of them got frightened. Golu ran towards a big tree and climbed on it. Poor Molu could not run fast and climb up the tree. But he showed his presence of mind. He had heard that bears did not eat dead bodies. So he lay down still on the ground and held his breath for a while, feigning himself dead. The bear came near Molu growling. He sniffed at his face and body. He took Molu to be a dead body and went away.

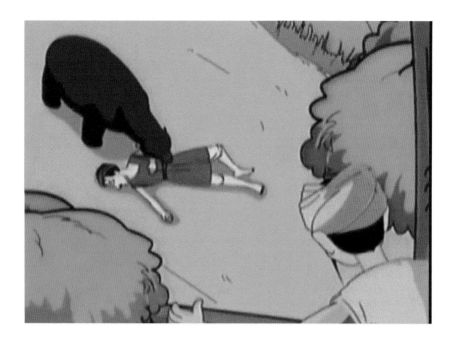

When the bear had gone away, Golu climbed down the tree. He went to Molu and asked, I saw the bear talking to you. What did he say to you, my friend?"

"Don't call me a friend", said Molu. "And that is what the bear also told me. He had said to me, 'Don't trust Golu. He is not your friend."

Golu was very ashamed. He felt sorry to have left his friend alone when in danger. Thus, their friendship ended for ever.

Moral: - *A friend in need, is a friend indeed.*

CHAPTER 36

THE FROG AND THE SERPENT

There lived a frog king in a deep well. His subjects and other relatives too lived in the same well. The relatives had an evil eye on his throne and often created problems for the king frog. In order to disrupt the smooth working of the kingdom, and with a view to cause impediments, they hatched a plan with the connivance of a minister of the kingdom and soon there was a revolt against the king frog. The king frog somehow managed to subdue the revolt, but he was very unhappy. He took a vow to take a revenge and teach them the lesson of their life.

One day, he came out of the well with the help of iron chains hanging on the walls of the well. He headed straight towards. The hole of a big serpent, which he had seen earlier.

Keeping himself at a considerably safe distance, king frog called out to the serpent. The serpent was surprised to hear a frog calling him. He came out of the hole.

"I wish to be your friend", said the king frog.

"But we are born enemies," replied the serpent. "How's it possible?"

"I will make it possible. I have a proposal," said king frog. He spoke to the serpent about his plan and told him that he was bent upon teaching his relatives a lesson. "I want to punish them. I will take you to the well and in the process you can eat them all."

"Is it a dry well?" asked the serpent.

"There is not much water in it", said the king frog. "However, you needn't worry. There is a nice hole in the wall of the well, a little above the water level. You can eat my relative frogs and retire into it to take rest."

"Okay, lead me to the well. I'll teach your relatives a lesson", said the serpent hissing loudly.

The king frog took the serpent to his well and said, "Here live my relatives and rebels. You can eat them all, but please spare my near and dear ones."

"All right," said the serpent and entered the well followed by the king frog. There he started eating the frogs, one by one, as and when pointed out by the king frog. Soon all the enemies of the king frog were eaten up by the serpent.

Now it was the turn of the king frog and his family. The serpent said to the king frog, "As you see, I've finished all your relatives and rebels. I've eaten your disloyal minister also. Now I've nothing to eat except you and your family."

King frog realized his folly. He had befriended his enemy to achieve his own selfish ends and settle his score with his enemies. The king frog felt as if death was in his hot pursuit. He, somehow, managed to gather some courage and said to the serpent, "No problem. I'll visit some other wells and ponds and persuade the frogs living there to resettle themselves in this empty well. Once they are in here, you can feast on them with ease."

"That's, good", the serpent became happy. "Do it soon. I'm hungry."

Both the king frog and his wife came out of the well and took to their heels, never to return to the same well again.

Moral: - *Never look to an enemy for help.*

CHAPTER 37

THE MONKEY AND THE CROCODILE

Long, long ago, there lived a huge crocodile in the river Ganges. The river flowed through a dense jungle. On both sides of the river there stood tall berry and other fruit trees. In one such tree there lived a big monkey by the name of Raktamukha. He ate fruits from the tree and passed his days happily jumping from one tree to another. Sometimes, he climbeded down the tree; took a bath in the river and rested for a while on its bank.

One day, the crocodile came out of the river and sat under the big berry tree in which the monkey lived. The monkey who was sitting high on a branch saw the crocodile taking a rest under the tree. He became very eager to talk to the crocodile and cultivate a friendship with him.

"Since you're taking a rest under the tree", said the monkey, "you'll be my guest. It's my duty to offer you food."

The monkey gave berries and other fruits to the crocodile to eat. The crocodile ate them and thanked the monkey for his hospitality. The monkey and the crocodile talked together for hours and soon they became friends. They developed such friendship that neither of the two was happy to miss each other's company even for a single day. Early since morning, the monkey would start looking for the crocodile, and the crocodile would also swim up to the berry tree as early as possible. They would sit together, have a hearty chat and the monkey would offer him the delicious berries. This became their daily routine.

One day, the monkey gave some fruits to the crocodile for his wife, as well. The crocodile took the fruits happily to his wife and also narrated the whole story to her.

The next day, the crocodile's wife said to her husband, "Dear, if these fruits are so tasty, then the monkey who eats these fruits must be ten times more tasty. Why don't you bring the heart of this monkey for my meals?"

The crocodile was shocked to hear these words from his wife. He said, "Darling, the monkey is my friend. It would not be fair to take his heart away from him."

"That means, you don't love me", said the crocodile's wife and began to cry.

"Don't cry, dear", said the crocodile. "I'll bring the monkey's heart for you."

The crocodile swiftly swam to the other bank of the river and reached the tree where the monkey lived.

"My wife and I invite you to our home for a dinner. My wife is very angry with me for not having invited you earlier," the crocodile said in a sad tone.

"But how will I go with you?" asked the monkey. I don't know how to swim."

"Don't worry", said the crocodile. "Just ride on my back. I'll take you to my house."

The monkey happily sat on the back of the crocodile and the crocodile started his journey in the water.

While in midstream, the monkey became frightened to see the water all around him and asked the crocodile to swim at a slow speed so that he did not fall into the river.

The crocodile thought that he could reveal his real intentions to the monkey, since it was impossible for him to escape from the middle of the river. So he said to the monkey, I am taking you to my home to please my wife. She wants to eat your heart. She says that since you eat tasty fruits day and night, your heart must be ten times more tasty than those fruits."

The monkey was taken aback to hear these words. He had never expected this type of a request from a friend. He kept his mental cool and said wittingly, "Very well friend. It would be my privilege to offer my heart to your charming wife. But alas! You didn't inform me earlier, otherwise, I'd have carried my heart with me. Which I usually keep in the hollow of the tree."

"Oh!" said the crocodile, "I didn't think of it earlier. Now we'll have to go back to the tree."

The crocodile turned and swam back to the bank of the river where the monkey lived.

Upon reaching the bank the monkey jumped off the crocodile's back and quickly climbed up his home tree. The crocodile waited for hours together for the monkey to return carrying his heart.

When the crocodile realized that the monkey was taking too long searching for his heart, he called him from the ground and said, "Friend, I believe, you must have found your heart by now. Now, please come down. My wife must be waiting for us and getting worried."

But the monkey laughed and said sitting at the top of the tree, "My dear foolish friend. You've deceived me as a friend. Can anyone take out his heart and keep that in a hollow. It was all a trick to save my life and teach a lesson to a treacherous friend like you. Now get lost."

The crocodile returned home empty handed.

Moral: - *At times, presence of mind pays well.*

CHAPTER 38

THE BRAHMIN AND THE THREE THUGS

Long, long ago, there lived a Brahmin in a small village. His name was Mitra Sharma. Once his father told him to sacrifice a goat according to some ancient rites. He asked him to visit the cattle fair in a nearby village and purchase a healthy goat for that purpose. The Brahmin visited the cattle fair and bought a healthy and fat goat. He slung the goat over his shoulder and headed back for his home. There were three thugs also roaming in the fair, with the sole intention of cheating the shopkeepers and other customers there. When they saw the Brahmin going back to his home with the goat, they thought of a plan to get the goat.

"This goat will make a delicious meal for all of us. Let's somehow get it. "

The three thugs discussed the matter amongst themselves. Then they separated from one another and took hiding positions at three different places on the path of the Brahmin.

As soon as the Brahmin reached a lonely spot, one of the thugs came out of his hiding place and said to the Brahmin in a surprised tone, "Sir, what's this? I don't understand why a pious man like you should carry a dog on his shoulders!"

The Brahmin was shocked to hear these words. He shouted back, "Can't you see? It's not a dog but a goat, you fool."

"I beg for your apology, sir. I told you what I saw. I am sorry if you don't believe it," said the thug and went away.

The Brahmin had hardly walked a hundred yards when another thug came out of his hiding place and said to the Brahmin, "Sir, why do you carry a dead calf on your shoulders? You seem to be a wise person. Such an act is sheer foolishness on your part."

"What!" the Brahmin shouted. "How do you mistake a living goat for a dead calf?"

"Sir," the second thug replied, "you seem to be highly mistaken in this respect yourself. Either you come from such a country where goats are not found, or you do it knowingly. I just told you what I saw. Thank you." The second thug went away laughing.

The Brahmin walked further. But again, he had hardly covered a little distance when the third thug confronted him laughing.

"Sir, why do you carry a donkey on your shoulders? It makes you a laughing stock", said the thug and began to laugh again.

The Brahmin hearing the words of the third thug became highly worried. 'Is it really not a goat!' He began to think. "Is it some kind of a ghost!"

The Brahmin got frightened. He thought to himself that the animal he was carrying on his shoulders might certainly be some sort of a ghost, because, it transformed itself from goat into a dog, from dog into a dead calf and from the dead calf into a donkey. The Brahmin was then terrified to such an extent that he flung the goat onto the roadside and fled.

The thugs caught the goat and feasted on it happily.

Moral: - *One should not be carried away by what others say.*

CHAPTER 39

THE KING AND THE PARROTS

Once a tribal king went to a jungle to hunt for birds. While hunting, he caught two parrots in his net. He was happy to catch the parrots as he could teach them to talk and then let his children play with the talking parrots. But while the tribal king was returning home with his two parrots, one of the parrots escaped from the net and flew away. The tribal king chased the parrot, but the parrot disappeared in the sky. The tribal king brought the other parrot home and taught it to speak like him. Soon the parrot learnt to talk like a tribal man.

The other parrot which had managed to escape, was caught by a sage. The sage liked the parrot and taught him to recite holy hymns. The sage lived at one end of the jungle, while the tribal king lived at the other end.

One day, a king of a nearby kingdom came in the jungle riding on his horse back. When he approached the tribal king's house, the tribal king's parrot shouted from inside the cage hanging outside the house, "Here comes someone. Catch this fellow and beat him up thoroughly."

The king hearing the parrot speak in such a filthy manner, left that place and reached the other end of the jungle where the sage lived. The sage's parrot was also kept in a cage, which was hanging outside the sage's cottage. As soon as the parrot saw the king approaching the cottage it said, "Welcome! Please come in and have a seat. What can I do for you? Have a glass of water. Eat some sweets."

After having welcomed him properly with all the etiquettes, the parrot called his master, "Sir, here comes a guest on his horseback. Take him into inside and offer him a seat. Serve him food."

The king was highly impressed with this intelligent talking parrot. He was quick to understand that good environment and training always yield a better result.

The tribal king's parrot spoke rudely, while the sage's parrot greeted him in a polite tone.

Moral: - *A man is known by the company he keeps.*

CHAPTER 40

THE REVENGE OF THE ELEPHANT

Long, long ago, there lived a big elephant in a small town. Despite his enormous physique, he was a very loving creature. People loved him and offered him delicious fruits to eat.

While going to the river to take a bath regularly he passed a tailor's shop. Tailor always gave him something to eat. The two became friends.

As usual one day, he put his trunk inside the shop. The tailor decided to play a prank on him. The tailor instead of giving him something to eat pricked a needle into his trunk. The elephant writhed in pain and sat on the ground. Some people gathered around him and began to laugh.

The elephant became angry and went to a nearby dirty pond. At the pond he collected some dirty water in his long trunk. On his way back he stopped at the tailor's shop, and emptied his trunk by spewing dirty water upon the tailor and all the clothes in the shop. All the clothes were destroyed. Thus the tailor had to suffer a heavy loss for his mischief.

Moral: - *Tit for tat.*

CHAPTER 41

THE LITTLE MICE AND THE BIG ELEPHANTS

Once upon a time a village was devastated by a strong earthquake. Damaged houses and roads could be seen everywhere. The village was, as a matter of fact, in a total ruin. The villagers had abandoned their houses and had settled in a nearby village. Finding the place totally devoid of residents, the mice began to live in the ruined houses. Soon their number grew into thousands and millions.

There was also a big lake situated near the ruined village. A herd of elephants used to visit the lake for drinking water. The herd had no other way but to pass through the ruins of the village to reach the lake. While on their way, the elephants trampled hundreds of mice daily under their heavy feet. This made all the mice very sad. Many of them were killed while a large number of them were maimed.

In order to find a solution to this problem, the mice held a meeting. In the meeting, it was decided that a request should be made to the king of elephants to this effect.

The king of mice met the king of elephants and said to him, "Your Majesty, we live in the ruins of the village, but every time your herd crosses the village, thousands of my subjects get trampled under the massive feet of your herd. Kindly change your route. If you do so, we promise to help you in the hour of your need."

Hearing this the king of elephants laughed. "You rats are so tiny to be of any help to giants like us. But in any case, we would do a favor to all of you by changing our route to reach the lake and to make you safer."

The king of mice thanked the king elephant and returned home.

After some time, the king of a nearby kingdom thought of increasing the number of elephants in his army. He ordered his soldiers to catch more elephants for this purpose. The king's soldiers saw this herd and put a strong net around the elephants. The elephants got trapped. They struggled hard to free themselves, but in vain.

Suddenly, the king of elephants recollected the promise of the king of mice, who had earlier talked about helping the elephants when needed. So he trumpeted loudly to call the king of mice. The king of mice hearing the voice of the king of elephants immediately rushed along with his followers to rescue the herd. There he found the elephants trapped in a thick net.

The mice set themselves on the task. They bit off the thick net at thousands of spots making it loose. The elephants broke the loose net and freed themselves.

They thanked the mice for their great help and extended their hands of friendship to them forever.

Moral :- *Never underestimate people by their appearance.*

CHAPTER 42

THE LION AND THE WOODCUTTER

There lived a lion in a dense forest. He had two good friends, a crow and a jackal. The lion hunted the whole day for his prey. And after assuaging his hunger, he gave the remaining food to his friends. The jackal and the crow were very happy to eat free food. They ate their fill and lazed around since they did not have to exert themselves to earn their food.

In the same village, there lived a woodcutter and his wife. Both husband and wife went to the forest to collect wood and returned home after hours of hard work. When they returned the woodcutter's wife cooked meals and they both ate sitting in front of their house.

Once the lion saw the woodcutter and his wife sitting outside the house and eating tasty meals. He could get the smell of the food from quite a distance. He went near them. The woodcutter and his wife, instead of running away from the spot, very courageously welcomed the lion and asked him to take a seat beside them. The lion was surprised. He sat beside the couple and happily ate the meals offered by the woodcutter. The lion was very pleased to see the hospitality extended by them and he was all-the-more pleased to eat and enjoy cooked meals.

This was the first time that he got the taste of cooked meals, otherwise he had always had raw meals in the past. While returning to the deep forest the lion thanked the woodcutter and his wife for the tasty food.

The woodcutter's wife said to the lion, "You're always welcome. Please do come everyday and share the food with us." Once again the lion was astonished. This kind of behavior was uncommon among them. The animals would never offer food to others; rather, they would snatch each other's food and injure each other in the process. The lion bowed before them with respect and went away. He took his lunch the next day also with the woodcutter's family. Gradually, he forgot to hunt for his prey and became lazy. This change in the lion's habits was a matter of worry for his friends, the jackal and the crow. In fact, his friends had to go hungry as they no longer got the leftovers of the lion's food. They decided to find the reason behind the change in his friend's attitude. So both of them decided to keep a watch on the lions' activities.

One day, they saw the lion sitting beside the woodcutter and having a good meal. They decided to meet the lion on the spot. But as soon as the woodcutter saw the jackal and the crow, he climbed up a nearby tall tree.

The lion was surprised by this reaction. The woodcutter said "Hey Lion, You are our friend. But since the crow and the jackal are cunning, I am protecting myself by staying out of reach from them."

Moral: - *Beware of cunning people.*

CHAPTER 43

THE HERMIT AND THE JUMPING RAT

On the outskirts of a small village, there was a temple, in which, there lived a hermit. He used to perform Pooja in the nearby villages. In the evening, after he had finished his meals, he would keep the remaining food, if any, into a bowl. He would hang the bowl upon a hook, which was attached to the ceiling by means of a string.

There, in the same temple, lived a fat rat. He was so fat that he didn't fear even the cats. He would come out of his hole during the night time and jump over to the hanging bowl and eat whatever food available in it. The next morning, when pundit would open the bowl, he would find it empty. This went on daily. The hermit became very sad. He didn't know how to drive the rat away from the temple.

Once a sage from another village came to stay with the hermit. The hermit had no food to offer to his guest. He became embarrassed and talked about his problem with the sage.

"Don't worry", said the sage. "We must find the hole where the rat lives and destroy it. The rat must have stored a large quantity of food in the hole. It's this hoard's smell that gives strength to the rat to make high jumps and reach the food bowl."

So the sage and the hermit together traced the rat's hole. They dug it up and destroyed the food stock stored there by the rat.

The rat becomes frustrated to see his food stock destroyed. He lost his vital energy to make high jumps. He had to go hungry now. He became weak due to hunger and came out in search the food. While he was running around in search the food the hermit spotted him. The hermit chased him and killed him with a stick.

Moral: - *The wealth gives only temporary strength.*

CHAPTER 44

THE WISE CRAB

There stood two big banyan trees, side by side, in a dense forest. In fact, they were at such a short distance from each other that they formed one huge banyan tree. Thousands of cranes lived in this tree. In a deep hole in its trunk, there also lived a big snake.

The snake used to climb up the tree to its branches and eat the baby cranes from their nests, when their parents were away in search of food. This had become a daily routine. And the unfortunate cranes were the soft targets. Every evening, on return to their nests, the hapless cranes would find their nestlings missing, and they were so helpless that they could not do anything to get rid of the big snake.

One day, a crab saw some cranes standing by the side of the lake and weeping bitterly. He asked them the reason of their grief. The cranes said, "There's a big snake living in the banyan tree. Every day he eats up our babies. We don't know how to get rid of him."

The crab thought to himself that the cranes too were crabs' enemies. They ate crabs' babies. Why not give the cranes an idea which not only would kill the snake but finish the cranes also.

So, the crab said, "Don't cry. I've an idea which will help kill the snake."
"Yes, please help us," requested the cranes.

"There is a big mongoose living at a little distance from the banyan trees. You put a few fish all along the path running from the mongoose's hole to the banyan tree. The mongoose will eat the fish one by one and then reach the snake's hole. Now you can yourself imagine, what will happen thereafter."

The cranes became very happy to get such a brilliant idea. They acted according to the plan.

Thereafter, the mongoose ate up all the fish put all along the path leading up to his home and then reached the banyan tree. There he found the snake in the hole. A fierce fighting took place between them and the mongoose killed the snake.

But instead of going back to his hole after killing the serpent, the mongoose further climbed up the tree and started eating the baby cranes, one by one. Soon the mongoose ate up all the baby cranes living in the banyan tree.

After eating a large number of baby cranes, the mongoose became very fat and lazy. One day, while he was sleeping on a branch of a tree, he slipped and fell onto the ground and died.

The crab was, thus, able to get rid of all his enemies.

Moral:- *Never act hastily on your enemy's advice.*

CHAPTER 45

THE SPARROW AND THE MONKEY

Long, long ago, there was a big banyan tree in a dense jungle. In this banyan tree, there lived a sparrow's family happily, with its nestlings. They had a beautiful and strong nest on a thick and sturdy branch of the tree. There was also a huge monkey living in the banyan tree. He had no house of his own to live in. Sometimes, he would sleep on one branch and sometimes, on the other.

Once it started raining very heavily. The rain was accompanied with thunder and lightening. Strong cold winds blew. There was not an inch of space left on the ground which was not lashed by the rain. While the sparrow's family protected itself from the fury of the rain by taking shelter inside the nest, the monkey could not find any safe place for himself. He began to shiver badly with the cold.

The sparrow seeing the monkey in such a pitiable condition said to him, "Poor fellow. Even though you are stout and healthy, you never built a house for yourself. Look at us. We have a beautiful and strong nest to protect ourselves from the fury of the rain and storm. Why don't you build a house for yourself, instead of wandering around aimlessly and shifting from one branch to the other in a lazy manner? God has given you two hands; make use of them."

The monkey, hearing the sparrow's words became very annoyed.

He said, "You foolish sparrow how dare you advise me, and teach me the do's and dont's of my life. You have lost your sense of etiquettes. I must teach you, how to behave with seniors." Saying so, the monkey tore off a branch from the tree and began to beat at the sparrow's nest.

Soon the nest was broken into pieces. The sparrows somehow flew away and took shelter on some other branch. They wept bitterly over the loss. They had no time even to repent for their good intentioned advice given to the monkey.

Moral: - *Never give advice to a fool.*

CHAPTER 46

THE STAG AND HIS ANTLERS

Once upon a time, there lived a stag in a dense forest. One day, he went to a nearby lake to quench his thirst. There he saw his reflection in the water and thought to himself; I've got beautiful antlers, but my legs are ugly. I can't understand, why God has given me such thin legs.

Just then, he heard a tiger roaring at a short distance. The stag knew that if he stayed there, the tiger will kill him. So he started running. The tiger too started chasing the stag.

The stag ran faster and faster and soon he outdistanced the tiger. But alas! All of a sudden, the antlers of the stag got entangled with the overhanging branches of a tree. The stag struggled hard, but could not free his antlers from the branches.

He thought to himself, 'My thin legs helped me get away from the danger, but my antlers proved dangerous for me.'

By that time the tiger had already reached there. He pounced upon the stag and killed him.

Moral: - *A beautiful thing might not be useful too.*

CHAPTER 47

THE FOOLISH DONKEY

Once upon a time, there lived a Washerman in a village. He had kept a donkey and a dog to serve as his pets. The Dog used to guard his master's house and escort him wherever he went. The Donkey used to carry stack of clothes on his back to and from the river. Both of them slept in the washerman's courtyard. Like this, they were leading their life under the kind shelter of the Washerman.

The man loved his dog very much. And the dog, whenever, he saw his master, would bark a little and wag his tail. He would raise his front legs and put them on the chest of his master. And the man would pat his dog in return, for his loving gesture.

This made the donkey jealous of the dog's fate. He cursed his ill-fate; 'What a bad luck I've. My master doesn't love me in spite of my putting in hard labor. Now, I must do what this dog does to please my master.'

So, the next time, when he saw his master coming, he ran towards him. He brayed a little and tried to wag his tail. He raised his front legs and put them on his master's body.

The man got frightened to see his donkey's abnormal behavior. He thought that the donkey might have gone crazy. So he picked up a stick and beat up the donkey till it fell on the ground.

Moral: - *Jealousy is harmful.*

CHAPTER 48

THE FALCON AND THE CROW

There lived a big falcon on a high mountain rock. Down in the plains, there lived a black crow in a huge tree.

One day, the falcon swooped down upon a baby lamb on the ground. The falcon caught hold of the lamb in his talons and flew back to his nest on the mountain rock.

The black crow saw the falcon do this thrilling feat. He thought to perform the same feat himself.

'What a fun it was to watch the falcon pick up the lamb from the ground! Now I'll myself do this.' The crow thought to himself and flew high in the sky. Then, he swooped down with great force upon a lamb grazing on the ground. But his swoop was not correctly aimed at and instead of catching the lamb, he dashed against a heavy rock . He died on the spot.

Moral: - *Never imitate others in a foolish manner.*

CHAPTER 49

THE TRADER AND THE SWEEPER

In a city called Vardhamana, there lived a rich trader by the name of Dantila. He was a prosperous merchant. He kept both the common man and the king very happy. He was respected and loved by all. Even the king respected him and had allowed him free access to the palace.

Dantila had a beautiful daughter. In course of time, her marriage took place. On this occasion, Dantila invited the entire public and the king and his courtiers.

A sweeper in the king's palace by the name of Gorambha, also attended the marriage . He sat beside the royal family members on a seat which was meant for somebody else. Dantila's men caught him by his neck and beat him up with a stick and told him to leave the place.

The sweeper felt insulted and decided to take revenge on Dantila.

Several days later, one early morning, when the king was not yet wide awake and Gorambha was on duty to sweep the place near the King's bed, he pretended to be drowsy and said, "This Dantila is a very cunning person. He poses as a gentleman, but, in fact, wishes to marry the queen."

When the king heard these words, he got up immediately from his bed and asked Gorambha, "Gorambha, is that true?"

"Master," said Gorambha, "when I am very much tired, I just mutter in my drowsiness. I don't know what I've been saying."

But the king was not satisfied with his answer. He thought, Gorambha was hiding some facts. From that day onwards the king withdrew his favors from Dantila. He was forbidden to enter the palace. Dantila was perplexed. He couldn't make out as to why the king's behavior had changed suddenly.

One day, Dantila and Gorambha came face to face outside the palace. Gorambha laughed sarcastically when he saw Dantila. Dantila quickly realized the reason behind the cold behavior of the king.

The next day, Dantila invited Gorambha to his house. He gave him a pair of garments and coconut and said, "My dear friend, I'm sorry for my behavior that day. But you must realize that it was entirely wrong on your part to take a seat, which was reserved for a guest. The guest felt insulted, and that is the reason why I'd throw you out. Please forgive me."

Gorambha was happy to receive the gifts. He said to Dantila. "Sir, Let us forget the past. This is my assurance that you will once again enjoy the favors of the king."

The next day, he went to the palace and started sweeping the floor. After some time, he again pretended to feel drowsy and when he became sure that the king was lying half awake, he muttered, "The king is very dirty. He eats cucumber in the toilet."

When the king heard this, he got up and sat straight on his bed and said to Gorambha, "What did you say, you stupid? When did you see me eating cucumbers in the toilet?"

Gorambha pretended as if he was frightened. "Your Majesty," he said in a quivering tone, "when I'm overworked, I feel drowsy during the daytime. I start muttering in my sleep. I've already told you about this. I really don't know what I was muttering."

When the king heard this, he was left in a profound thought: "This Gorambha is an idiot. He mutters lies in his sleep. As I've never eaten cucumber in the toilet, so in the same way it is quite possible that Dantila too had never had any bad desire."

After having considered this carefully, the king invited Dantila to the palace. He presented him with jewels and clothing and Dantila's former status was regained.

Moral: - *No one is high or low. So we must never insult anyone.*

CHAPTER 50

THE WOLF AND THE CRANE

Once, there lived a greedy and cunning wolf in a dense forest. One day, while he was having his dinner, a bone got stuck into his throat. He tried hard to take it out, but couldn't succeed in his effort.

The wolf began whining with pain. The pain was unbearable. The wolf got worried and began thinking, "The pain will subside in due course. But, what will happen if the bone doesn't come out. I won't be able to eat anything. I will starve to death."

The wolf began thinking of some possible remedy to overcome the problem.

Suddenly he recalled that there was a crane who lived on the banks of a nearby lake. He immediately went to the crane and said, "My friend, I've a bone stuck deep into my throat. If you could please pull it out of my throat with your long beak, I shall pay you suitably for your help and remain ever-grateful to you."

The crane saw his pitiable condition and agreed to help him. He put him long beak, and in the process, half of his neck also, deep into the throat of the wolf and pulled the bone out. The wolf was very happy to have the bone pulled out of his throat.

"Now pay me my fees, please," The crane requested.

"What fees?", said the wolf. "You put your head into my mouth and I let it out safely. That's enough of my kindness. Now get lost, otherwise, I'll harm you."

Moral: - *Be careful of wicked people.*

CHAPTER 51

THE THIEF, THE GIANT AND THE BRAHMIN

Long ago, there lived a poor Brahmin in a village. He used to perform Poojas in the nearby villages to earn his living. Once a rich farmer gave him a cow and told him to sell cow's milk in the market to earn part of his livelihood. But the cow was very weak. The Brahmin then begged for alms and fed the cow. Soon the cow became fat and healthy.

Once a thief saw the fat cow of the Brahmin and decided to steal it. One night he headed towards the Brahmin's house.

A giant also used to live somewhere near the village. He devoured human beings. The thief met this giant, while he was on his way to the Brahmin's house to steal his cow.

The thief asked "Who are you and where are you going?".

The giant replied, "I'm a giant. I eat humans. Today I'm going to devour the Brahmin. But who're you by the way?"

"I'm a big thief. I steal whatever I like. Today, I've decided to steal the Brahmin's cow."

"Come on then!" said the giant. "Let's go together to the Brahmin's house."

So, both of them reached the Brahmin's house together. The Brahmin was deep asleep at that time. The thief whipped out a big knife from his pocket and started walking to the place, where the cow was tethered. But the giant blocked his way.

"Wait friend!" the giant said. "First let me eat this Brahmin."

"No!" said the thief. "It's quite possible that while you go to eat the Brahmin, he wakes up and runs away. In that case there might be quite a commotion here and as a result, neither you'll get your Brahmin nor will I get my cow."

And thus, both of them started having a heated argument between thems. The loud arguments woke up the Brahmin. He soon realized the whole situation.

He recited mantras and burned the giant with his spiritual powers. Then he started beating the thief with a long and thick stick. The thief began to cry and ran to save his life.

Thus, the Brahman was saved from both of them.

Moral: - *Quarreling on any issue always benefits the others.*

Dedicated to Teju, Shashank, Nihira, Nandu, Avani, Yadhu and Vaishu.

If you liked this book, you might also enjoy: -

Panchatantra 40 More Stories with Moral (Illustrated)
ASIN: - B00B7OICDU

We also have a series "10 stories from Panchatantra" with below volumes: -

1) Book 1 – Discord Among Friends
ASIN: - B00BC04BFM

2) Book 2 - Gaining Friends
ASIN: - B00BC02TTW

3) Book 3 – Of Crows and Owls
ASIN: - B00BC3GPAI

4) Book 4 - Loss of Gains
ASIN: - B00BC5AEYO

5) Book 5 - Imprudence
ASIN: - B00BC2C1S4

We welcome your feedback / comments / suggestions. Our email i.d :-

VYANST@GMAIL.COM

THE END

Made in the USA
Lexington, KY
25 April 2015